BARRY HUTCHISON

INVISIBLE FIENDS

THE CROWMASTER

HarperCollins *Children's Books*

First published in paperback in Great Britain by
HarperCollins *Children's Books* 2011

HarperCollins *Children's Books* is a division of HarperCollins*Publishers* Ltd
77-85 Fulham Palace Road, Hammersmith, London W6 8JB

Visit us on the web at www.harpercollins.co.uk
Visit Barry at www.barryhutchison.com

Text copyright © Barry Hutchison 2011

ISBN 978-0-00-731517-8

Barry Hutchison reserves the right to be identified as the author of the work.

Printed and bound in England by Clays Ltd, St Ives plc

To Ewan.

INVISIBLE
FIENDS

THE CROWMASTER

Watch the birdie!

For my big sis, Carol Anne.

Sorry for turning your Bucks Fizz record into a clock.

But it was 18 years ago.

Let it go.

PROLOGUE

What had I expected to see? I wasn't sure. An empty street. One or two late-night wanderers, maybe.

But not this. Never this.

There were hundreds of them. *Thousands.* They scuttled and scurried through the darkness, swarming over the village like an infection; relentless and unstoppable.

I leaned closer to the window and looked down at the front of the hospital. One of the larger creatures was tearing through the fence, its claws slicing through the wrought-iron bars as if they were cardboard. My breath fogged the glass and the monster vanished behind a cloud of condensation. By the time the pane cleared the *thing* would be inside the hospital. It would be up the stairs in moments. Everyone in here was as good as dead.

The distant thunder of gunfire ricocheted from somewhere

near the village centre. A scream followed – short and sharp, then suddenly silenced. There were no more gunshots after that, just the triumphant roar of something sickening and grotesque.

I heard Ameena take a step closer behind me. I didn't need to look at her reflection in the window to know how terrified she was. The crack in her voice said it all.

'It's the same everywhere,' she whispered.

I nodded, slowly. 'The town as well?'

She hesitated long enough for me to realise what she meant. I turned away from the devastation outside. 'Wait... You really mean *everywhere*, don't you?'

Her only reply was a single nod of her head.

'*Liar!*' I snapped. It couldn't be true. This couldn't be happening.

She stooped and picked up the TV remote from the day-room coffee table. It shook in her hand as she held it out to me.

'See for yourself.'

Hesitantly, I took the remote. 'What channel?'

She glanced at the ceiling, steadying her voice. 'Any of them.'

The old television set gave a faint *clunk* as I switched it on. In a few seconds, an all-too-familiar scene appeared.

Hundreds of the creatures. Cars and buildings ablaze. People screaming. People running. People *dying*.

Hell on Earth.

'That's New York,' she said.

Click. Another channel, but the footage was almost identical.

'London.'

Click.

'I'm… I'm not sure. Somewhere in Japan. Tokyo, maybe?'

It could have been Tokyo, but then again it could have been anywhere. I clicked through half a dozen more channels, but the images were always the same.

'It happened,' I gasped. 'It actually happened.'

I turned back to the window and gazed out. The clouds above the next town were tinged with orange and red. It was already burning. They were destroying everything, just like *he'd* told me they would.

This was it.

The world was ending.

Armageddon.

And it was all my fault.

NINETEEN DAYS
EARLIER...

Chapter One

BROUGHT TO LIFE

The house was quieter than I ever remembered it being. The stairs didn't creak as I tiptoed barefoot down them. The kitchen door didn't make a sound when I edged it open. Even the fridge, which usually gives a strange gurgle when anyone so much as touches it, stayed silent as I pulled back the door and blinked in the faint orange glow of the light.

The floor was cold beneath my feet. I curled my toes in and tried to balance on my heels, minimising contact between my skin and the chill of the lino. I'd been given slippers at Christmas, but in all the... *excitement* of the day, they'd got lost.

The shelves of the fridge were almost bare. Tomorrow

was shopping day – well, technically, since it was after midnight, today was shopping day, but since I hadn't been to sleep yet I was still classing it as 'tomorrow'. Pity. There was never anything decent in the fridge on the day before shopping day.

The milk carton felt light when I picked it up and carried it across to the table. If I drank some there probably wouldn't be enough left for cereal in the morning. I grabbed a glass from the draining board and half filled it anyway. Nan always said milky drinks were good for helping you get to sleep, and drinks don't come much milkier than milk.

On the wall above the microwave the plastic hands of the clock crept past 3 a.m. There were no ticks, no tocks, just the same flat silence that seemed to have fallen like a blanket across the world.

I put the carton with its dribble of milk back in the fridge and closed the door. It gave a gurgle, but it was short and faint, and nowhere near its usual high standard.

With glass in hand I wandered through to the living

room, where the carpet slowly warmed the soles of my feet. The lamp post outside spilled light through a gap in the curtains – not much, but enough to help me avoid most of the room's major obstacles.

Lifting the remote control from the top of the TV I made for the couch. I wasn't sure what television stations filled their night-time slots with, but it had to be more interesting than lying on my back staring at the ceiling until morning.

Sipping my milk, I sat on the couch and curled my legs up beneath me. The TV came on at the first press of the remote, and the silence was suddenly shattered by a loud, nasal laugh. The sound made me jump, and a splosh of milk slid up the side of the glass and spilled down the sleeve of my pyjamas. The thumb of my other hand frantically searched for the mute switch.

At last I found the button. The laughter was immediately cut short. I sat there with the remote still pointed at the television, breath held, listening for any sign that I'd woken anyone up.

Not a bedspring groaned. Not a floorboard creaked.

Gradually, my muscles began to relax and I leaned back against the cushions. The milk had trickled down past my elbow, but was now being absorbed into my PJs, so at least I didn't have to worry about cleaning it up.

On the TV, the laughing man was still guffawing away, only now I couldn't hear him. I recognised him as a chef from one of the cookery programmes that Mum watches. He and another man were in a room filled with big wooden barrels and racks of wine bottles. Every so often they'd fill a glass, take a sip, spit it back out into a bucket, then start laughing again like a couple of maniacs. I'd tasted wine on Mum's birthday a few months ago. It tasted like vinegar and left a horrible film on my tongue. No wonder the men on the telly were gobbing the stuff out rather than drinking it. I'd been tempted to do the same thing myself.

In the bottom-right corner of the screen, a little woman was making a series of frantic hand gestures. I knew she was signing for the deaf, but I didn't understand why whenever the men on screen laughed, she pretended to laugh too.

What was the point in that? Surely deaf people could see the men were laughing? They didn't need her shaking her belly and contorting her face into a big Santa-Claus-style chortle, did they?

I flicked over to another channel. A skeleton-faced man with a long white beard was looking at an even longer mathematical equation on a whiteboard. I quickly hit a button on the remote and moved on.

The next programme I found was about Egypt. The pyramids were a dead giveaway. Someone was signing for the deaf on this channel too. This time the person doing the sign language was a man. He looked very excited about being on telly. His face moved as if it was made of living Plasticine, and his hand gestures were so wild and frantic he looked in danger of slapping himself unconscious. Every movement and gesture he made was ridiculously exaggerated. I wondered if that was how deaf people shouted at each other.

I watched the strange animated little man until I'd finished the rest of my milk. He was far more interesting than the actual programme and I could have kept watching him all night, but I was yawning now and it felt like sleep might be at least a vague possibility.

I hit the red button on the remote and the picture on screen turned into a thin line of colour, then disappeared completely. Pushing with my legs I bounced up off the couch and took a few steps towards the kitchen.

Something hidden by the gloom on the floor snagged my foot. I barely had time to realise it was one of Ameena's boots before I stumbled, staggered, then started to fall.

I managed to catch the edge of the coffee table, but still came down hard on my knees. The jolt of my abrupt stop shuddered through me, and I felt the wet glass slip from my fingers.

Crash. The milky tumbler smashed against the wooden tabletop, showering it and the carpet in a hundred sharp crystalline slivers. The shattering sound shook me to the core, and not because I was worried about getting into trouble. It was because the sound had reminded me of something – something I'd been trying hard to forget.

The last time I'd heard glass break had been here in this very room. That time it hadn't been a drinking glass smashing, though. It had been the window, as my childhood imaginary friend, Mr Mumbles, came crashing through.

Kneeling there on the floor I could remember it all so clearly. The panic as the window came in. The shock as Mr Mumbles fixed me with his beady glare. The sight of him. The smell of him. The feeling of his rough hands around my neck.

My throat tightened as I pushed myself up on trembling legs. I could hear the faint murmurings of movement upstairs now. Someone had heard the glass breaking. A feeling of relief washed over me, easing the knot in my stomach. The memory of my all-too-real imaginary friend had disturbed me, and right at that moment I really didn't feel like being alone.

And then I realised.

I wasn't alone.

He was standing there in front of the curtains, just as he

had been last time. His wide-brimmed hat curved down, hiding his face in a mask of shadow. His heavy overcoat swished softly back and forth on a breeze I couldn't feel or hear. His stench hit my nostrils; the familiar stink of filth and decay and of things long dead. It caught way back in my throat and made me gag.

He tilted his head and the light from outside pulled the dark veil from his face. There was the cracked, papery skin. There were the narrowed eyes; the hooked nose, through which his foul breath came whistling in and out.

And there, stretched into a humourless smile, were the lips – thick and bloated, and criss-crossed by a series of short grubby stitches that sealed his mouth tight shut.

My head shook all by itself, trying to deny what my eyes were seeing. But there was no avoiding it. There was no other way of explaining away what I was looking at. I didn't know he'd done it, but he had. Somehow he'd come back.

Mr Mumbles was back.

Again.

'Kyle?' I heard Mum's voice at the same time the living-room light came on.

'Mum, move, get out!' I cried, spinning quickly to face her. She was standing at the bottom of the stairs, dressing gown wrapped around her, a finger still on the light switch.

'What?' she frowned. 'Why? What's wrong?'

'It's him,' I spluttered, turning back to the window. 'It's... *Wait*. Where did he go?'

'Where did who go?'

'Mr Mumbles,' I yelped. 'He was there. By the window!'

'What? Are... are you sure?'

'Of course I'm sure,' I told her as I began to search the room. 'He was right there when you switched the light on.'

'I didn't see anyone. It was dark, are you sure—?'

'He was *there*, OK?'

Mum stood in silence, watching me check behind the curtains, the couch – anywhere Mr Mumbles might be hiding.

'What's all the ruckus?' asked Ameena, who had now appeared behind Mum. She was wearing the pyjamas

Mum had bought for her, and an old dressing gown of Nan's. This was the fourth night Ameena had slept here, but I still hadn't got used to seeing her. The sight of her knocked my train of thought, and Mum replied before I could.

'He thinks he saw Mr Mumbles,' she explained.

'I don't *think* I saw him, I *did* see him!' I dropped to my knees and looked under the coffee table. It was a long shot, but I checked just in case.

'Well unless he's eight centimetres tall I doubt he's under there,' Ameena said.

'What, you think this is funny?' I demanded. 'Have you forgotten what he did to me? To all of us?'

'No, I haven't forgotten,' she said defensively, 'but—'

'But what? But *what*?'

'Look, chill out,' she told me. 'If he *was* here then he's not here now.'

'Ameena's right,' said Mum before I could reply. 'Let's just all go back to bed and we can talk about it in the morning.'

I looked at them both in turn, barely able to believe what I was hearing.

'Are you *nuts*?' I cried. 'I'm telling you I just saw Mr Mumbles and you think it can wait till morning?'

'I know that's what you think you saw,' Mum continued, 'but I was standing right here and I couldn't see anyone.'

'He was here!' I insisted. 'He was right here! What, was I imagining him or something, is that what you're saying?'

Mum didn't speak, but her face said it all.

'I dunno,' Ameena shrugged. 'I saw what happened to him up on the roof, and I don't think that's something you come back from. Even if you *are* an imaginary evil monster guy.'

I glanced between them, still amazed at what I was hearing, but fully aware I wasn't going to win this argument. Not against both of them.

'Fine,' I scowled, 'let's all go back to bed. But if you both get murdered in your sleep, don't come crying to me in the morning.'

* * *

I'm not sure how long I lay there on my bed, propped up against my pillows. An hour? Two? The world outside was still wrapped in darkness and morning felt like a long way away.

I hadn't been able to relax since returning to my room. I was certain I'd seen Mr Mumbles, but the more time passed the more unbelievable that seemed. Mr Mumbles was dead. Very dead. You couldn't get much deader. But I'd seen him.

Hadn't I?

What if he hadn't been there? Could it have been that I'd been dreaming somehow? Or hallucinating? The lack of sleep and the flashback of the breaking glass could have sent my imagination into overdrive. It was possible, I supposed. And Mum must've been there for at least a few seconds before she switched the light on, yet she hadn't seen anyone in the room besides me.

I felt the muscles in my back relax a little. The headache that had been pulsing behind my eyes since I'd come back to bed eased off a few notches. Maybe Mum and Ameena were right. Maybe I was worrying about nothing. Nothing that a few hours of sleep wouldn't fix, anyway.

A glance at my bedside clock told me it was barely after four. School had been closed for the past few days while investigators tried to work out how every pupil and teacher had managed to develop temporary amnesia at exactly the same time; so I could sleep on for as long as I wanted.

I closed my eyes and allowed myself a smile. I could still remember the looks of panicked confusion on the faces of the teachers and students as they 'awoke' to find themselves standing in my front garden. The police and the school inspectors and anyone else who fancied could investigate all they liked. There was no way they'd figure out the truth. It was just too weird. There was no way they'd ever find out about—

The soft giggle from the end of my bed seemed deafening in the silence. My childhood instincts screamed at me to pull the covers over my head and hide, while my more grown-up ones ordered me to sit up and face whatever was with me in my room.

In the end I came up with a compromise. I kicked off the covers and rolled out of bed, pushing myself into the corner of the room and as far from the source of the sound as possible.

A small, frail figure stood watching me from the gloom. Her flowing white dress was caked thick with dried blood. In her hands she clutched a dirty porcelain-faced rag doll. Raggy Maggie's single eye bored into me as the girl waved one of the doll's stubby arms up and down.

'Peek-a-boo,' sang Caddie. 'I see you!'

Chapter Two

OF MONSTERS PAST

Silence filled the room like a void. Caddie was still standing at the foot of my bed, still making the doll wave at me. Her dark eyes watched me, unblinking, but she made no attempt to move closer.

A thousand thoughts crashed together in my head. I reached out and plucked one at random.

'How did you get here?'

She didn't answer.

'What are you doing here?' I demanded – more loudly, but not loud enough to wake anyone up.

'She doesn't want to play with us any more,' the girl spoke softly.

I hesitated, trying to figure out the meaning behind her

words, if there even was one.

Caddie looked just like she'd done four days ago. The smear of lipstick was still a red blur across her lips. Her face was still a rainbow of badly applied eyeshadow and blusher and whatever other names they give to make-up. Beneath it all her skin was still as pale as bone, and her lifeless stare still gave me the willies.

'*Who* doesn't—'

'Oh, you remembered,' she said. Her face broke into a wide smile.

Again I paused. 'Remembered what?'

'She won't play any more,' Caddie said, apparently fighting back tears. 'We were having so much fun, but then she just wouldn't play.'

Confusion had taken over from terror now. I had no idea what the girl was talking about, although there was something about her words that seemed familiar.

'S'not fair,' she muttered. 'Every time I find a new friend to play with they get broken.'

Broken. A circuit connected in my brain and I realised

why I felt like I'd heard this before. I *had* heard it before. Caddie was repeating everything she'd said to me in the school canteen – the first time I'd seen her here in the real world. I remembered Mrs Milton, my head teacher, lying on the floor. Sobbing and babbling. And broken.

I ran back over the meeting in my head. If I could remember what she said next then I could prove to myself I was right. What was it she'd said? What had *I* said? Something about Billy.

'Not telling,' she spoke.

Of *course*, that was it.

'I told you, silly, I'm not telling,' I blurted out, as quickly as I could. She started to speak before I was half finished.

'I told you, silly,' she giggled. 'I'm not telling!'

It was as if I was looking at a recording. Every word, every inflection of her voice was exactly like it had been in the school. Any second now she'd ask me if I wanted—

'Tea?' she enquired.

And now I thought about it I realised it wasn't just Caddie. When Mr Mumbles appeared on Christmas Day

I'd first seen him in front of the living-room window. He'd stood there, hat pulled down, coat swishing in the breeze, beady eyes boring holes in mine.

He'd looked exactly the same when I saw him again tonight. The same stance in the same position in the same room. It was as if my encounters with both him and Caddie were being somehow replayed or re-enacted.

I detached myself from the corner of the room and cautiously moved towards the bed. Caddie's eyes followed me, but she made no other movement. She was still talking – telling me I'd get a cake if I was extra good – but I was no longer really listening.

The bedsprings squeaked when I stepped up on top of the mattress. It was impossible to walk around the bed without having to go through Caddie and her doll, but I could go over it and reach the door without having to pass too close to them.

I thudded down on to the other side of the bed. The closed bedroom door was just a few steps away now. My eyes remained locked with Caddie's as I backed towards it, my hand searching for the handle.

'Raggy Maggie likes sugar, don't you, Raggy Maggie?' was all she said as I slipped out on to the upstairs landing.

The door to Ameena's room was directly across from mine. It used to be where Nan slept when she lived with us, but – apart from Christmas Day – it had been empty ever since she'd gone into the old folks' home a few years back.

The door wasn't fully shut. I nudged it open and took a backwards step inside. My eyes were still on Caddie. I didn't want to let her out of my sight for a second, in case she pulled a vanishing act like Mr Mumbles had.

I could hear Ameena's breathing, soft and slow. She was asleep. Not for long.

'Ameena,' I hissed into the gloom. 'Ameena, wake up.'

I heard her gasp quietly. The bed gave a sharp creak as she sat quickly upright. 'What?' she said, more loudly than I'd have liked. 'What's wrong?'

'Come here, quick.'

'What is it?'

'Just come and look!' I hissed, giving her an imploring

look. She muttered faintly beneath her breath as she threw off her covers and came to join me by the door.

She needn't have bothered. The spot where Caddie had been standing was empty. I cursed myself for glancing away.

'Gone,' I said. 'She's gone.'

'Who's gone?'

'Caddie.'

'Yeah, four days ago,' Ameena said.

I shook my head. 'No, not four days ago. Now. A second ago.'

I marched across the landing and into my room. Empty. Ameena sauntered in behind me.

'You were probably just dreaming.'

'I'm telling you she was here,' I said, pointing to the foot of my bed. 'Standing right there.'

Ameena opened my wardrobe door and peeked inside. 'Not in there,' she said, closing it again with a *click*. 'You sure you weren't dreaming, kiddo?'

I flopped down into a sitting position on my bed. First

Mr Mumbles and then Caddie. What was happening to me?

'I saw her,' I said, my voice coming out as a quiet croak. 'I saw her as clearly as I'm seeing you.'

'Maybe you just imagined—'

'No,' I snapped, 'she was here.'

'You didn't let me finish. I'm not saying she wasn't here, I'm saying maybe you imagined it.'

I looked up at her and blinked, even more confused than I had been. 'How do you mean?'

'Remember in the garage?' she said. 'When we fought Mr Mumbles. You told me you thought about a light coming on, and what happened?'

'A light came on,' I frowned, 'but—'

'And you thought how handy it would be to have a weapon, didn't you? And then...'

'I found the axe.'

'Exactly,' she nodded. 'So what happened downstairs? Just before you saw Mr Mumbles.'

'I dropped a glass,' I told her.

'And?'

I hesitated, having already realised the road this conversation was taking me down. 'And I remembered him coming through the window.'

'And I'll bet just before your other guest turned up you'd been thinking about her too.'

I looked from Ameena to the spot where Caddie had been standing. Though I didn't realise it, I must've nodded.

'Thought so,' Ameena said. She looked pleased with herself. I felt like she'd just kicked me in the stomach.

'So, what,' I began, 'every time I remember them they're going to come back, is that it? Every time I think about what happened they're going to come leaping out of the shadows?'

'There's a simple solution.'

'What's that?'

'Don't think about them.'

Easy for you to say, I thought, but I didn't say it out loud. I looked down at the floor. Was this it? Was I doomed to a life of running from ghosts of monsters past? I had to know.

One way or another I had to find out for sure.

'You might be right,' I nodded, standing up.

'Of course I'm right. I'm always right.'

'But let's do a test,' I suggested.

Ameena's eyes narrowed in suspicion. 'What kind of test?'

'I'll think about one of them and see if I can make them appear.'

Ameena didn't say anything for a moment. I saw her look over at my bedside alarm. The LED display told her it was well before five. She sighed as she realised she wouldn't be getting back to bed any time soon. 'OK,' she nodded. 'Let's give it a try.'

'Close the door,' I instructed. I bounced up and down on the spot a few times, taking four or five big, deep breaths.

'Ready?' Ameena asked.

I stopped bouncing and nodded. 'Ready.'

We stood there for a long time, neither one of us saying anything, until Ameena eventually broke the silence.

'You started yet?'

I winced. 'I don't know which one to think about.'

'Good grief,' she muttered, shaking her head. 'Think about whatever one scared you the least. I don't want you freaking out on me if you do make them appear.'

'Right,' I said. 'Good idea.'

I closed my eyes. It was a close-run thing, but I found Mr Mumbles marginally less scary than Caddie, even though it probably should have been the other way around. There was a vague familiarity to Mr Mumbles that Caddie didn't have, and I think that's why he didn't terrify me quite as much as the girl with the doll did.

Lost in the blackness behind my eyes, I tried to picture my old imaginary friend. It wasn't hard. He had a face that wasn't easy to forget, and I'd seen it up close so many times it was burned into my memory for ever.

Almost straight away, Mr Mumbles stumbled from the fog inside my head, arms outstretched, hands clawing at thin air. Instinctively I opened my eyes and pulled away, although there was nothing to pull away from. Only Ameena and I were there in the room.

'What happened?' she asked.

'I thought about him,' I said. 'I could picture him coming at me.'

'And what about now?' she asked, casting her eyes around the room. 'Can you see him now?'

I shook my head. 'Maybe I should try again.'

'If you like,' Ameena nodded, before she gave a yawn so big it threatened to swallow her own head.

'Let's try in the morning,' I suggested, taking the hint. 'It's late. Or early, depending on how you look at it.'

'Good call. You be OK?'

'Course,' I said with a smile, as I guided her towards the door. 'I'll be absolutely... Wait. Did you hear something?'

We stood listening to the silence.

'Nope.'

I hesitated, then reached for the door. For a moment there I'd thought I heard...

'Footsteps,' I whispered. 'Listen.'

We leaned closer to the door. Ameena stared down towards the end of her nose, the way she always did when she was listening hard.

Thup. The sound of the footstep on the hallway carpet was almost too soft for us to hear. Almost.

Ameena's eyes met mine. She gave a brief nod and we both stepped back from the door.

Thup.

'Now do you believe me?' I whispered as I looked around for something to use as a weapon. The only thing close to hand was a pillow, and I couldn't see that being a lot of help.

Thup. The footsteps stopped right outside the bedroom door. Ameena and I both took another step away.

I narrowed my eyes and gave the power sleeping inside me a nudge. At once I felt the familiar tingling sensation creep across my scalp; saw the flashes of blue and white sparks across my vision. When Mr Mumbles stepped through the doorway he'd be stepping straight into a world of pain.

Standing shoulder to shoulder, I felt Ameena tense as the handle of the door slowly began to turn. The dull metal gave the faintest of *creaks* as it was pushed all the way down.

The electricity buzzed through my skull. I raised my hands, not yet sure what I was going to do to Mr Mumbles, but certain it was going to be something nasty.

The door edged open and a head appeared through the gap. Mum looked half asleep. She also looked angry.

'What's going on?' she demanded, pushing the door the rest of the way open. 'It's the middle of the night.'

'Mum,' I breathed, feeling the tingling in my head subside. 'It's only you. We thought it was—'

He stepped out behind her without a sound, raising the axe before I could grasp what was happening. Everything seemed to lurch into jerky slow motion as Mr Mumbles swung his arm round in a wide arc. I heard Ameena give a yelp, and watched, helpless, as the blade of the axe sliced through the air.

And straight towards Mum's neck.

Chapter Three

A GOODBYE

I have no memory of moving. I don't remember hurling myself at Mr Mumbles, or how I managed to reach him before the axe could find its target.

All I remember is my shoulder hitting him hard in the chest and the sound of the air leaving his body in one short sharp breath.

We tumbled, a flailing ball of arms and legs, through the door into Ameena's room. He was laughing before we hit the floor, that low, sickening cackle I'd heard too many times before.

My fist glanced off his chin. He didn't flinch. Kept on laughing. I brought the sparks rushing across my head. Pictured my muscles bulging. Faster. Stronger.

Bam. The next punch twisted his head around. That shut him up, but I hit him again anyway, across his crooked nose this time. It split with a *crack*, spraying thick black blood on to the carpet.

This time I was getting rid of him for good. There would be no coming back from what I was about to do to him.

How many times did he try to strangle me at Christmas? Four? Five? I'd lost count of how often I'd felt his hands around my throat. Now it was my turn. My fingers wrapped around his windpipe and I pushed down with all my weight. His eyes bulged and his grey skin took on a purple hue as I choked whatever passed for life out of him.

I heard a sound on the carpet right behind me. *Caddie*, I thought, releasing my grip and twisting at the waist. The lightning zapped through my brain before I knew what was happening. Mum was lifted off her feet and driven backwards into the wall. It shook as she slammed against it, hard enough to send some of Nan's old ornaments toppling from their shelves on the other side of the room.

I was on my feet at once, Mr Mumbles forgotten. Ameena

was at Mum's side before I was, kneeling down, checking she was OK. Mum groaned and edged herself into a seated position against the wall. Her face was contorted in pain, but there was something else there in her eyes when she looked at me. Something I'd never seen before.

Fear.

'Mum, are you all right? I'm sorry,' I spluttered. 'I didn't know it was you. I thought...' My words wilted under her gaze. 'You saw him, right? You saw him?'

She nodded, but her eyes didn't leave mine, and the expression behind them didn't change.

'He's gone,' Ameena said, standing up and searching the room. 'Where did he go?'

We were right by the door. There was no way he could have got out that way, but Ameena ventured on to the landing to check anyway. She returned a second later and gave a shrug.

'Disappeared,' I said. 'Like before.'

'You were going to kill him,' Mum breathed.

'I had to,' I told her. 'He was going to kill you.'

Mum's eyes searched my face, as if seeing it for the first time. 'But the way you flew at him. The way you were hitting him...' Her eyes went moist and she looked down at my hands. Mr Mumbles' blood still stained my knuckles.

'You were going mental,' Ameena said. I shot her a glare, but she fired it straight back. 'We were shouting at you to stop. Didn't you hear us?'

I nodded unconvincingly. I hadn't heard a thing.

Mum winced as she tried to stand. Ameena and I both held out a hand to help her up. She looked briefly at mine, then took Ameena's.

'What's the problem?' I asked, more aggressively than I meant to. 'I had to do it. I had to stop him. Don't you get that?'

'Downstairs,' Mum said, placing her hands on her lower back and giving her spine a stretch. 'You and I need a little talk.'

'But, Mum—'

'Downstairs, Kyle,' Mum said, not angry but sad, which was worse. 'It wasn't a request.'

I sat in the kitchen, listening to the cheeping of the birds outside, and the distant rumblings of the first of the early-morning traffic. Mum's 'little talk' had become a long discussion, and although it was still mostly dark outside, the clock on the wall told me it was almost seven.

The hot chocolate Mum had made an hour ago had gone cold. It sat in a mug on the table in front of me, untouched. I was too stunned to drink any of it. Too shocked by what Mum was suggesting to do anything but fight back the tears that were building behind my eyes.

'It's for the best,' Mum said. My gaze was lowered to the table. I could see her hand resting on top of mine, but I couldn't feel it.

It's for the best. She'd said those words nine times during our two-hour conversation. Only *It won't be for long* challenged it for the coveted title of Most Overused Phrase. They had been neck and neck almost the whole way through, but this last instance had pushed *It's for the best* into a nine-eight lead. It was nail-biting stuff, and concentrating on the game was probably the only thing that was stopping me from crying.

'I'm sorry, Mum, it was an accident,' I said croakily, raising my eyes to meet hers. 'Don't do this, please.'

'I promise, sweetheart, it won't be for long,' smiled Mum weakly.

Nine all.

'It won't happen again, I swear.'

'It's not that you hurt me. That's not what I'm worried about,' she said. 'I'm worried about you. And Ameena. And... and *everyone*. If you've started making those... those *things* come back, then no one's safe. No one.'

Part of me knew she was right. If I was somehow making the enemies I'd faced return, it would be dangerous for anyone to be around me.

Another part of me was even more worried, though. Mr Mumbles was dead. Caddie was dead. There shouldn't have been anything left of them to come back.

Could it be that by picturing them so vividly I was somehow *creating* them? Was my imagination bringing them to life? It sounded impossible, but everything I'd been through in the past few weeks had made me take a long hard look at my definition of "impossible".

Despite all this, despite everything I knew and everything I suspected, there was one thing keeping me from agreeing with Mum's plan.

'But... I don't want to.'

She squeezed my hand and glanced towards the window. Before she turned away I saw the softness in her eyes. A butterfly of excitement fluttered in my belly as I realised she wasn't going to go through with it. She couldn't.

When she turned back, though, her expression had changed. The softness was still there, but a wall of determination had been built in front of it.

'I'm sorry, Kyle,' she said in a voice that told me the debate was now over. 'But you're going to have to leave.' She gave my hand another squeeze, before adding: 'It's for the best.'

Ding ding, I thought, as the first of the tears broke through my defences and trickled down my cheek. *We have a winner.*

Four hours later I was on a train, wedged in tight against

the window by one of the fattest men I'd ever seen in my life. The carriages were all pretty busy, and I had considered myself lucky to find a seat at all. Now, jammed there with my arms pinned to my sides and my face almost touching the glass, I wasn't so sure.

He'd joined the train at the stop after mine. From the second he squeezed himself into the carriage I knew he'd end up next to me. There were two or three other seats free, but I knew my luck wasn't good enough for him to choose one of those. Sure enough, he heaved himself along the aisle until he was level with my seat, then plopped down next to me with a heavy grunt. No matter which way you looked at it, this really wasn't shaping up to be a good day.

The track clattered by beneath us; a regular rhythm of *clackety-clack, clackety-clack*. The train shifted left and right on its wheels. Every time it swung left I found myself squashed further by the bulk of the behemoth beside me.

It was an hour or so to Glasgow, where I would have to get off this train, go to another station, and get on a second train. Then it was nearly three hours until my stop, where I would be met by Mum's cousin, Marion. From there it was a ten-mile drive to Marion's house, where I would be living for at least the next month.

Mum had shown me the place on the map. It was a remote little house located slap bang in the middle of nowhere. Apart from the train station there seemed to be nothing within twenty miles in any direction. Mum had described it as 'perfect'. I guessed 'painfully dull' would probably be much more accurate.

I still didn't want to go, but Mum's reasoning for sending me to Marion's did make sense, I had to admit.

It was our house, she said. Huge chunks of the horrors I'd experienced in the past few weeks had taken place in the house, and Mum believed just being there was what was making the bad memories so vivid. Vivid bad memories, it seemed, led to very bad things happening.

She reckoned being around her and Ameena could also be contributing. It was just after she said this that she dropped the bombshell about going to live with Marion. She hoped the change of scene would help me to stop conjuring up anything that might try to kill me. I'd probably just die of boredom instead.

Marion didn't have any children, which was another reason for sending me there. Mr Mumbles had been my imaginary friend, and Caddie had been Billy Gibb's – a boy from my class in school. If they only came back when the child who imagined them was around, then taking me away from children should keep me safe from any more homicidal visitors. At least, that was the theory.

'Nice view.'

The huge man in the seat next to me was leaning into my space, admiring the scenery as it whizzed by the window. His face was red and sweaty, as if he'd just completed a marathon. He was completely bald, and as he breathed I could detect a definite whiff of milk. Stick him in a giant nappy and you could have passed him off as the world's largest baby.

I quickly pushed the thought away. The last thing I needed was for that mental picture to become a reality too.

'Yeah, it's nice,' I replied, looking out at the fields.

'See the little birdies?' he asked, jabbing a podgy finger against the window. 'Pretty.'

Ignoring the urge to point out to him that he wasn't talking to a three-year-old, I followed his finger. A large flock of black birds was flying parallel to the train, about thirty or so metres away. They moved as one, all soaring in perfect time together, as if taking part in some carefully orchestrated dance.

'How are they keeping up?' I mumbled, not really expecting an answer. 'We must be doing eighty miles an hour.'

'They're crows,' he said, as if that somehow explained things.

'Are crows that fast?'

He made a sound like air escaping from a balloon. *SS-SS-SS-SS*. It took me a moment to recognise the sound as laughter. 'Them ones are.'

I kept watching the crows. I doubted they could keep up this pace for long. Any second I expected them to fall back and be left behind by the train, but they remained level for several minutes. If anything, they seemed to be pulling ahead a little, although I couldn't be certain of that.

'Where you off to?' The man-baby's voice was close by my ear and I gave a little jump of fright. We were so close he must have felt my sudden jerk, but he didn't let on if he did.

'Glasgow,' I said, not wanting to give away too much information.

'Big city,' he said. Every word he spoke seemed to make him more and more breathless. I realised that was why he used as few of them as possible. If a sentence had more than four words in it he had to stop for air halfway through. 'Shopping?'

'Something like that.'

'Young lad. On his own. Big city,' the man wheezed. 'Dangerous.'

'I'll be meeting friends,' I lied. I was keeping my gaze pointed out of the window, hoping he'd take the hint.

'Yes. You will be.'

I turned to face him, struggling against the bulk of his

arms. 'Sorry? What did you say?'

'I'm sure you will be,' he panted. 'Meeting friends, I mean.' His mouth folded into a gummy smile and I realised for the first time that he had no teeth. Maybe he really *was* the world's biggest baby.

'Tickets, please.'

I was glad the ticket collector chose that moment to appear. Anything to save me from having to talk to the weirdo next to me.

I felt like a circus contortionist as I tried to squeeze my hand down between the man and me so I could reach into my pocket. He must have realised what I was trying to do, but he made no attempt to make things easier. *Bad baby,* I thought, and I couldn't help but smile.

My ticket was a little crumpled when I finally managed to haul it from my pocket. I straightened it out as best I could before holding it up for the ticket collector.

'Sorry,' I said, 'it got a bit squashed.'

'No problem,' the collector said. He clipped a hole in the ticket, then handed it back to me. As I reached out to take it I almost yelped with surprise. The ticket collector turned and moved along the aisle, but not before I caught sight of his face and realised who he was.

I'd seen him three times before. Once in the police station when I'd been chased by Mr Mumbles, then twice at the school when I'd faced Caddie and Raggy Maggie. I had no idea who he was, but as I watched him move along the train I knew one thing for certain.

I was going to find out.

Chapter Four

JOSEPH

'Excuse me, can I get past?'

The mega-baby scowled at the question. 'Why?'

'I need to see the ticket collector,' I said with some urgency in my voice. The man-of-mystery didn't seem to be bothering with anyone else's tickets, and was instead walking casually along the train to where a sliding door led through to the next carriage.

With a sigh of annoyance and a grunt of effort, the obese man shifted his immense weight in the seat. His breath became laboured as he caught hold of the headrest in front of him and began to ease himself upright. Huge flaps of blubber wobbled below his arms like fleshy wings. His face contorted in effort as he pulled himself into a standing position.

I moved to pursue the ticket collector, but the bulk of my fellow passenger still blocked the aisle.

'I'm up,' he grunted. 'Might as well go to the bog.'

I pushed my fist into my mouth to stop myself shouting in frustration. The toilets were in the same direction as I was trying to go, and there was no way of squeezing past the waddling beast of a man. I had no choice but to follow behind as he plodded his way along the train, his massive girth brushing against the seats on either side of the aisle.

He was too big even to see past. I hopped into the air a couple of times, but his height and the sheer expanse of his back stopped me seeing if the ticket collector was still in the carriage.

After what felt like a decade we arrived at the end of the compartment, where the aisle widened a little. I squeezed my way past the man and hit the control for the door. It slid open with a *shhht* and I hurried through. Behind me, the mega-baby forced his bulk through the door and stopped by the toilets.

'If you're not back,' he managed to wheeze, though he sounded like the effort might kill him, 'window seat's mine.'

I nodded without looking back. My luggage was in a rack at the end of the train and I had left nothing in my seat. Now that I was free, I had no intention of going back to sit there.

I heard the toilet door close and lock, and tried hard not to imagine the horrors about to be unleashed inside that unsuspecting little room.

A glass door led into the next carriage. I could see right along that aisle and the next one, where the train ended. There was no sign of the ticket collector anywhere.

My hand was halfway to the button that would swish open the door when a voice to my right stopped me.

'Looking for someone?'

I hadn't noticed anyone standing in the little alcove where the exit door was, and my shock must've been visible on my face when I whipped round. The ticket collector gave a self-satisfied smirk, as if he'd been deliberately trying to surprise me.

'You, actually,' I said, recovering quickly.

He nodded and pushed back his hat, revealing a head that was almost – but not quite – as bald as the man-baby's. 'Well, you found me.'

The ticket collector was short and a little on the podgy side. He looked to be around sixty, but stood with the type of slouch usually reserved for teenagers. It rumpled his uniform and made it look two sizes too big. He smoothed the edges of his thick, bushy moustache while he waited for my reply.

'Who are you?' I asked, unable to come up with a less obvious question.

'Ticket collector,' he said with a smile. 'Tickets, please. See?'

'Who are you really?'

'I told you, I'm a ticket collector,' he insisted. 'Always have been.' I opened my mouth to argue, but he kept talking. 'Just like I'm a policeman and always have been. And just like I will for ever be standing behind the curtain in your school canteen, waiting to untie you.'

I blinked slowly. 'Nope,' I said. 'You've lost me.'

'It's OK,' he chuckled, 'it's not easy to understand. It'll be years before you figure it out. Forty-four, to be exact.'

My brow was knotted into a frown. I'd come looking for answers, but all I was getting was gobbledegook. 'Right,' I stumbled. 'So... who are you?'

'The ticket—'

'What's your name?' I sighed, growing tired of this. The man across from me, on the other hand, seemed to be enjoying every second.

'I've got lots of names.'

I glared at him. 'Pick one.'

He thought for a moment. 'Kyle Alexander.'

'That's my name,' I said.

'Oh yes,' he said with a wink. 'So it is. How about... Joseph?'

'Joseph. Joseph what?'

'Just Joseph will do for now,' he smiled.

The door next to me slid open and a woman came through. She was about my mum's age, and looked almost as strung-out as Mum had looked as she'd waved me goodbye. A boy of around three was in the woman's arms. He fiddled with her long hair, not paying us the slightest bit of attention.

The woman gave us a faintly embarrassed smile as she made for the toilet door.

'Out of order, love,' Joseph announced. 'Sorry. The one further along's fine, though.'

A flicker of irritation flashed on the woman's face, but she thanked him and carried on along the train.

'Why did you tell her it's out of order?' I asked.

'Because it will be in a minute,' Joseph answered. I assumed he was anticipating a big clean-up job when the mega-baby finally emerged. 'Now I need to get back to work,' he told me. 'Lots of tickets needing to be collected today. Was there anything else?'

I had too many questions to ask. They buzzed like a swarm of bees inside my head – one big collective noise that was almost impossible to break down into its component parts.

I fumbled for words. 'Just... just... everything. What's happening to me? What's going on?'

'Wow, straight for the biggies then,' Joseph said, sucking in his cheeks. 'What do *you* think is happening?'

'I don't know!' I cried, launching into a full-scale rant. 'That's why I'm asking you. First my imaginary friend comes back and tries to kill me, then someone else's appears and tries to do pretty much the exact same thing. I find out my dad's actually my mum's imaginary friend, and, I mean, I don't even want to begin to think about how that's even biologically possible. I've suddenly got these... these... *powers*, and now it's like either they're going crazy or I am, because everywhere I look I'm seeing Mr Mumbles or Caddie or... or...'

'Or me?'

'Right,' I said, my tirade running out of steam. 'Exactly. Or you.'

Joseph nodded thoughtfully, his eyes studying the smooth lines of the train's ceiling. He gave a final nod and turned back to me.

'Yep,' he said.

I waited expectantly for him to continue. 'Yep what?'

'Yep,' Joseph said, 'that's pretty much what's happening to you. Couldn't have put it better myself. You hit the nail right on the head.' He glanced at his watch. 'Now, if you'll excuse me—'

'What, *that's it?*' I spat. 'You're not going to tell me anything else?'

'I think you'll do a fine job of figuring it out all by yourself.'

He tipped his hat towards me and made for the door that led to the next carriage. I watched him, dumbstruck.

'I thought you could help me,' I told him. 'I thought that was why you were here.'

He paused at the door. For a long moment there was no sound but the *clackety-clack* of the train on the track. When Joseph finally spoke, the lightness was gone from his voice.

'I am helping you, Kyle,' he said. 'I'm doing everything I can.'

'Not from where I'm standing.'

He turned round and straightened from his slouch. There was an intensity to his expression that seemed to change the entire shape of his face.

'You think so?' he asked, his voice flat and emotionless. He nodded towards the door to the toilet cubicle. 'Look in there.'

'What?' I gasped. 'No way! There's someone in there.'

'You sure?'

'Yes! I saw him go in. Couldn't exactly miss him.'

'There's a window,' Joseph said.

I snorted. 'What, are you saying he's climbed out? *That guy?*'

One of Joseph's eyebrows raised so high it almost disappeared beneath the brim of his hat. 'I'm not saying he went anywhere.'

Joseph took a pace forward and swiped a credit-card sized piece of plastic across the face of the door control button. The light around the switch blinked from an occupied red to a vacant green. 'Go on,' he urged, stepping away. 'Open it.'

I looked from the door to Joseph and back again, my mouth flapping open and closed like a fish out of water. 'You can't be serious!'

'You say I'm not helping you. That I'm doing nothing. I'll show you,' Joseph said. There was an authority to his voice I'd never heard before, even when he'd been dressed as the policeman. The bumbling oaf persona had slipped away, revealing a much more commanding presence lurking behind it. 'Open the door,' he said. 'Open the door and see how I help you.'

'By showing me fat people on the toilet?' I muttered, but I was already staring at the circle of green. Already knowing I was going to do it. Already reaching for the button.

The door clicked off the catch as my finger brushed over the switch. The toilet door didn't slide sideways like the others and I had to give it a push to start it swinging inwards.

The smell that rushed out to meet me stung my eyes and caught in my throat. My gag reflex kicked in and I had to pull my jumper up over my nose and mouth to stop myself throwing up.

As the door swung all the way open I felt my whole body go rigid. The sight I had expected to see when I opened the toilet door had been bad enough. The sight that did greet me was worse. Beyond worse.

Way, way beyond.

What was left of the mega-baby lay twisted on the floor, the vast flapping limbs contorted into impossible positions, the head bent awkwardly sideways, as if his neck was made of rubber.

He was slumped on the lino like a big wobbly blob. There was no rigidity to him. Nothing solid. It was as if something had crawled inside him and devoured every one of his bones. All that remained was a mound of blubbery skin. It swayed hypnotically with the movement of the train.

The man's mouth was wide open, but his eyes were wider. They looked beyond me, devoid of life, but pleading for… I don't know. Mercy or dignity or *something*.

There wasn't a spot of blood anywhere on the floor or

the walls. A broken window was the only sign of a struggle. The hole in the glass would have been too small even for me to fit through, so I didn't know how it fitted in with the rest of the grisly scene.

My eyes met with his again, and I suddenly felt very ashamed for thinking so badly of the poor guy. I stood there, transfixed by the man's mushy remains, until Joseph reached forward and swung the door closed.

I blinked, the spell broken. 'He's... he's... dead,' I whispered.

Joseph swiped his card across the door control button and the lock blinked red. 'Well spotted,' he said. 'What gave it away?'

'What did you do to him?' I asked, missing the sarcasm completely.

'Me? Nothing. I've been standing here with you. Nothing to do with me.'

'Then what happened?'

'Long story,' Joseph said. 'And one you're probably best not knowing for the moment. I'll clean it up. I'll take care of it. That's what I do. That's how I help you, Kyle. I tidy things away. I tie up the loose ends.'

I nodded, my eyes still fixed on the door. I couldn't get the sight of the man's remains out of my head. I think I muttered 'OK', but I couldn't say for certain.

'Go back to your seat,' Joseph told me. 'Try to act natural. You'll be in Glasgow before you know it.'

I nodded again, too numb to do much else. The door to my left slid open and Joseph gave me a nudge to start me moving along the aisle.

Just before I started to walk, he put a hand on my shoulder. He may have been a small man, but his grip was like steel. 'One thing you should ask yourself,' he said, his voice quiet so no one else would hear. 'Did that man die *after* he went into the toilet, or *before*?'

The hand withdrew from my shoulder and I stood in the mouth of the aisle, waiting for the sentence to filter properly through to my brain.

'After,' I frowned, turning on the spot. 'I saw him walk...'

I left the rest of the sentence hanging in the air. The area around me was empty. Joseph had pulled his usual disappearing trick.

I skulked along the aisle back to my seat. I kept my gaze on the floor, avoiding all eye contact for fear of somehow giving away what I'd just seen. As I walked, all I could hear was Joseph's final question, repeating over and over again in my head like the steady clattering rhythm of the train on the tracks.

Of course he'd died *after* going into the toilet. I'd watched him walk in. But the way Joseph asked the question, and the fact he'd even asked it at all, made me wonder if he knew something about the man-baby that I didn't.

Chapter Five

MEETING MARION

The change at Glasgow had gone smoothly enough, once I'd managed to find the other train station. It was hidden down a side street, and I'd arrived just as the dozen or so passengers were boarding the train.

The carriage I was in was virtually empty, and I'd found a seat with no problems. We pulled out of the station just a minute or so after I sat down. I gazed out through the grimy window, watching grey concrete tower blocks trundle slowly by. After the fifteenth or sixteenth identical block had passed, I settled back in my seat and closed my eyes.

Immediately I was confronted by the pleading stare of the mega-baby. Lost in the darkness behind my eyelids, all I could see was his wide face, wobbling atop his mushy remains like melted ice cream. His rubbery lips flapped open and shut, but no sound came out, just the choking stench of sour milk.

I opened my eyes again, and knew at once that I'd been dreaming. The housing estates had been replaced by rolling expanses of greens and browns. They stretched off in all directions, becoming trees and hills and lochs in the distance. The scenery where I live is pretty impressive, but the sights I saw through the train window were picture-postcard beautiful.

I'd sat there, admiring the view and slowly waking up, for something like ten or fifteen minutes. Eventually, a robotic-sounding female voice had announced we would soon be arriving at my stop.

As I heaved my bag down from the overhead luggage rack, I felt an uneasiness in the pit of my stomach. I may have left some dangers behind when I'd boarded the first train that morning, but who knew what waited for me up ahead?

* * *

Nothing. That was what waited for me. Nothing and no one.

The station was almost exactly how I imagined it would be – an old stone hut with a flimsy plastic shelter attached to one crumbling wall. There was also a clock mounted on the wall, but its hands were stopped at eleven fifteen. Moss grew around the clock's face, so I'd be surprised if the hands had stopped at eleven fifteen any day recently. It had probably been frozen like that for months, if not years.

I listened to the clattering of the train growing fainter, and wondered what I should do next. Marion was supposed to be at the station to meet me, but besides the building itself, there was nothing but hills and trees for miles around.

I thought about phoning Mum. She'd given me the mobile phone she'd been keeping for my birthday, and topped it up with some credit so I could get in touch whenever I wanted. I think she was trying to reassure me she wasn't just sending me away and cutting all contact.

And then I remembered that the phone hadn't been

charged up yet. The battery was completely flat, so calling anyone wasn't an option. It didn't matter. Marion was probably just held up somewhere. Stuck in a traffic jam or something.

My eyes wandered along the dusty, single-track road that led away from the station. *Traffic jam*, I thought. *Yeah, right*.

My bag almost knocked me off balance as I swung it up on to my shoulder. I immediately swung it back down again, realising I may as well leave it beneath the plastic shelter while I went for a look around. It wasn't like it had anything worth stealing in it, and even if it had, there was nobody around to steal it.

The steps leading down from the platform were little more than cleverly arranged boulders. I picked my way down them, holding on to the rough stone wall of the station building for support.

There was no path at the bottom, but a track had been worn through the tangle of grass and heather that surrounded the building. A soft wind swished through the foliage, and I realised its whispers were the only sound I could hear.

I was completely alone – further away from any other human being than I had ever been in my life. There was nothing but me, the landscape and the flock of birds circling far, far above my head. It was strangely relaxing.

The track curved around the back of the station building. I followed it, almost skipping along, until I realised I wasn't actually alone at all.

A battered old Morris Minor estate car stood in the small car park behind the station. The building shielded the four-space parking zone, making it impossible to see from the platform.

The car was dark blue, with occasional spots of brown rust. Its entire rear end was clad with panels of varnished wood, giving the impression it was half car, half walk-in wardrobe.

I knew right away it had to be Marion's. I couldn't remember much about Mum's cousin, but I remembered enough to know this was exactly the type of thing she was likely to drive.

The front door swung open and my suspicions were confirmed. Marion's prematurely grey head popped up on the other side of the roof. One of the few things I could remember about her was the colour of her eyes. They were a striking shade of bright blue. They almost shone as she fixed me with a glare, gave me a curt nod, then stared down at my empty hands.

'No luggage?'

'What? Oh. Um, hi, Marion,' I smiled. 'I left my bag up there. I didn't think...'

She nodded again and climbed back into the car. The door closed behind her with a *thunk*.

'I'll just go and get it, shall I?' I muttered. I waited for a moment to see if she'd pop back up. She didn't, so I turned and backtracked up to the platform.

When I got there I found another surprise waiting for me. An oily-black crow sat perched on top of my bag. Its wings were folded in against its back, and its head was tilted slightly to one side. The bird's dark, beady eyes stared at me as I scurried up the stone steps and stopped.

'Shoo,' I said, stamping my foot hard on the ground. The bird didn't flinch. I took a few steps closer and stamped my foot again, harder this time. The crow tilted its head further to the side, but otherwise did nothing.

We watched each other for almost a minute, while I tried to figure out what to do next. I'm not keen on birds, not since the budgie we had when I was three got its claws tangled in my hair. My memory of the thing flapping and pecking at my head as it tried to get free is hazy, but even now, when I get up close to anything with feathers, I can feel myself getting nervous.

And the monster perched on top of my bag was no budgie. For a start it must've been about fifty centimetres in length. Its beak was long and curved, with short feathery tufts covering the top. Its legs were long and spindly, tapering at the bottom into sharp-looking claws.

The feathers, the legs, the beak; no part of the bird was any other shade but black. It didn't just look like a crow, it was a perfect example of *crowness*. Like something from a creepy fairy tale. Or – I realised with a shudder – a horror story.

'Right, come on, shift,' I urged, clapping my hands loudly and shuffling towards my bag. The bird gave a faint *caw*, then hopped into the air. It appeared to beat its wings only once, but that was enough to carry it up to the roof of the station building. It perched there, watching with its dark eyes, as I picked up my bag and made my way back to Marion's car.

'You got it then,' Marion said, as I clambered into the passenger seat. The inside of her car was as neat and tidy as it was chilly. I slipped my seatbelt on and pulled my jacket tightly around me. Somehow it felt colder inside the car than it did outside.

'Yep,' I replied, fighting to stop my teeth chattering together.

'Right then,' she said, cranking the engine. After four or five attempts it spluttered noisily into life. 'Let's be off.'

Marion was twenty years and a few months older than my

mum, which made her fifty-one. If you didn't know, you'd swear she was pushing seventy.

Her hair had gone grey in her late thirties, Mum had told me. Others might have tried to disguise it with dye, but not Marion. She wore it scraped back into a tight bun. It wasn't the best-looking hairstyle in the world, but like everything about Marion, it was efficient.

We had been travelling for almost ten minutes, the car swerving to avoid some potholes, and bouncing through those that slipped under Marion's radar. We had travelled in silence for most of the way. Marion hadn't said a word since she'd started driving, and I realised it was going to be down to me to break the ice.

'So,' I began, hunting for something to talk about, 'the scenery's nice.'

Marion shrugged and made a short grunting sound.

The suspension creaked as the old car thudded through another pothole.

'How far is it to your house?' I asked.

'Twenty minutes.'

'Oh, right,' I said, nodding. 'Twenty minutes.'

'That's right.'

I turned towards the side window. Despite the cold inside, the glass had started to steam up. I wiped the condensation away with my sleeve, but it made the glass streaky and difficult to see through.

'Nice car,' I ventured. 'Had it long?'

'Too long,' she said. 'But I paid for it honestly. Not that you'd know anything about that.'

I frowned. 'What's that supposed to mean?'

'Well,' she said, sucking in her cheeks, 'coming up here, running away. "Trouble", that's what your mother said you were in. Only one kind of trouble I can think of that'd send you running up here. Law-breaking trouble.'

'Wait... you think I'm in trouble with the police?'

'I should have told her "no",' Marion continued. 'I don't know what I was thinking. Harbouring a fugitive. At my age. But family's family, and Lord knows your mother's had a hard enough time of it.'

'Marion, I'm not... I haven't done anything wrong. I'm not

a wanted criminal or anything.'

She tore her eyes from the road for a fraction of a second and met my gaze. 'Aren't you?'

'No!' I exclaimed. 'It's… just some problems with a kid in school. Bullying, really.' I smiled, even though I wasn't pleased with myself for lying to her. 'That's all.'

She drove along in silence for a few hundred metres. 'Oh,' she said at last. I could see her tight grip on the wheel relaxing. 'I see.' A flicker of warmth passed across her face and her thin, colourless lips curved into a smile. 'Well then, why didn't you say?'

'You didn't ask,' I replied, pleased to see her smiling.

'That's a very fair point,' she conceded. She took a deep breath and let it out in a big sigh of relief. 'Well, that is good news. I was thinking you'd been up to all sorts. Let my imagination run away with me no end. You ever find yourself doing that?'

I hesitated before replying. 'It's been known to happen.'

'I'll have to take the scratchy blankets off your bed when we get back,' she said. 'Put on some nice soft ones.'

'You gave me scratchy blankets?' I laughed. 'That's just nasty.'

'I thought you were a crook,' she said, her smile widening. 'I was teaching you a lesson. You should have seen the slop I was planning serving up for dinner. A few days of eating that and you'd have been begging to be sent to prison.'

'Cunning plan,' I said. I was beginning to warm to Marion now that she wasn't treating me like a murder suspect. 'Except for one flaw.'

'What's that?'

'It'd probably still have been better than Mum's cooking.'

For a second I thought Marion was going to sneeze, but instead she erupted into gales of laughter. It was a loud, infectious laugh, and I found myself joining in.

'Good point!' Marion guffawed. 'I hadn't thought of that. Is she still as bad as she—'

'Look out!'

KA-RASSHK!

The windscreen splintered into a wide spider-web pattern as something smashed against it. Marion stopped laughing instantly.

Her foot shifted to the brake and pushed down hard. The tyres spat out dust and gravel and the car spluttered to a stop.

We tried to look outside, but the cracks ran from one side of the glass to the other, making it impossible to see through. Whatever had hit the windscreen had hit it hard.

'What happened?' gasped Marion. Her hands were shaking and her face was pale. 'What was it? Did someone throw something?'

'I don't... I'm not sure,' I said. 'I saw something, and then it just...'

Marion recovered from the shock before I did. She quickly unclipped her seatbelt, pushed open her door and clambered out.

By the time I got out of the car, she was standing up in front, peering down at a lifeless black shape on the bonnet. She clicked her tongue against her teeth, then turned to look at me.

'It's a crow,' she said glumly. I peered down at the mangled remains of the bird. 'Nothing to worry about. Just a silly old crow.'

Chapter Six

LOST

'Well, this is a first. This is a first for me,' muttered Marion, as she traced a fingertip along one of the windscreen's cracks. The bird was still on the bonnet, its neck bent back and its beak hanging wide open. 'I've never known one to do that before.'

'What, never?' I asked.

Marion shook her head. 'We get a lot of low-fliers round here, and I've hit my fair share of them, but usually they just skite off the glass, no real harm done.' She plucked a black feather from one of the cracks, studied it briefly, then let it float to the ground. 'This one must have been going like a bat out of you-know-where to do damage like that. Silly little beggar.'

'Are there a lot of them round here?' I asked. 'Crows, I mean.'

'Hundreds. Thousands. Hundreds of thousands, probably. Used to terrify me when I was a girl until a friend of mine showed me they were nothing to be afraid of,' replied Marion, turning her attention to the bird itself. It was on its side, with its legs buckled outwards in opposite directions. One wing was trapped beneath its body, while the other was bent right back above its head. From where I was standing, it looked like it was sniffing its own armpit. Or wingpit, if you wanted to get technical about it.

It reminded me again of the man-baby in the train toilet. All the right component parts, but violently rearranged into something disturbing and unfamiliar. I shuddered and tried to forget the image.

'Should I get a stick?' I asked.

Marion looked at me with a puzzled expression. 'Whatever for?'

'To, you know, flick it off the car with,' I said, miming the action.

Marion's hands wrapped around the bird. Its head

flopped even further back as she lifted it, until its lifeless eyes were staring straight at me. 'Or we could just, *you know*, pick it up,' she said with a smirk.

'Or we could do that.'

She walked over to the edge of the road. 'We'll have to knock the windscreen out for now,' she said. 'Might be a bit draughty, but at least we'll be able to— Ow!'

The crow hit the ground with a soft thud. Marion's hand flew to her mouth, but not before I saw the tiny river of blood trickling between her index finger and thumb.

'What happened? Are you OK?'

Marion was sucking the wound on her hand, and staring down at the bundle of black feathers at her feet. 'It pecked me,' she gasped, pulling her hand from her mouth to assess the damage. 'The ruddy thing lifted its head and pecked me!'

I stepped closer and gave the bird a prod with my toe. It didn't move or do anything else to suggest it was still alive.

'Must've been a nerve twitching or something,' I

suggested. 'Like when you chop a chicken's head off. Its body keeps running around.'

Marion raised her eyebrows. 'You've chopped a chicken's head off?'

'No, no, I haven't, but I've heard that's what happens. I read it somewhere, I think. Must have been something like that, because look.' I gave the crow another poke. It rolled limply on to its back. 'Nothing.'

Marion's gaze shifted from me to the crow and back again. She shook her head faintly and gave me a smile. 'Of course it must,' she said, already striding back towards the car. 'Now come on, you can help me knock out this windscreen.'

Marion's house stood by itself at the edge of a dense forest of towering pine trees. The building looked old, but well cared for, with clean white paint on the rough stone walls, and a neat stack of firewood piled up by the back door.

A large garden was fenced off at one side of the house. Most of it seemed to be just soil, but there were rows of evenly spaced greenery dotted here and there. A crooked path of yellowish brickwork led down to an ancient-looking greenhouse at the far end of the plot.

An identical pathway led up to the house from the wide driveway where Marion had parked the car. I clambered from the passenger seat and stood on the path, half admiring the impressive old building, half waiting for Marion to lead the way inside.

'On you go then,' she prompted, nodding towards the back door. 'Follow the yellow brick road!'

I hauled my bag higher on my shoulder and began along the path. 'You've got a nice big garden,' I said.

'Veg mostly, but not really the season for much at the minute,' Marion replied. 'It's only fenced off to make it more manageable.'

She gave a vague wave of her hand. 'Most of the land from the road up to the woods belongs to the house. Too much for me to look after, so I marked out something a bit less... overwhelming.'

'You grow your own vegetables?'

'Of course! I'm quite self-sufficient up here,' she said proudly. 'Really not much but leeks and sprouts ready at the minute, though. Fancy either of those?'

I shook my head. 'No, thanks.'

'Don't know what you're missing,' Marion scolded, and for a moment she reminded me of Mum. 'Anyway,' she continued, as we reached the back door, 'in you go. Watch out for Toto. He'll probably come leaping out at you.'

'Toto?'

'My dog,' she explained, opening the door. 'He's... Oh.' She looked around the kitchen. 'He's not here. Must be off roaming. He'll come back at dinner time, no doubt.'

I stood just inside the back door, taking in the large kitchen. It had wood on the walls and tiles on the floor. An old, complicated-looking cooker seemed to take up half of one wall, boxed in by a mismatched assortment of storage units on either side.

A rack of pots and pans hung from the ceiling, too high for anyone to reach. A thin rope led from the rack, across the yellowing ceiling, and down to a hook on the wall. I guessed that was how Marion lowered the pots enough to get to them. Either that or she kept a pair of stilts handy.

There were two windows – one large, the other much smaller. There were no curtains, but each window had its own set of wooden shutters that could be closed across it. I didn't imagine Marion shut them often. I couldn't see how she could have any privacy problems way out here.

A folding table was pushed against one wall, with a single wooden chair tucked in underneath. I could imagine Marion sitting there, eating her meals alone, with only Toto for company. Suddenly – despite her huge house with its sprawling plot of land – I found myself feeling sorry for her.

'Well, this is it,' she said, almost bashfully. 'It's not much, but it does me well enough.'

'It's really nice,' I assured her. 'Much bigger than our kitchen at home.'

'Too big, probably,' Marion said. 'Now come on. I'll give you the grand tour.'

* * *

I lowered myself carefully on to the bed, trying it out. Marion hadn't been kidding about the scratchy blankets. They were made of a coarse, grey material that may well have been a cross between camel hair and barbed wire. Fortunately, she had swapped them for different ones within two minutes of us stepping through the bedroom door.

The blankets I sat on now were made of a soft fleecy material. They felt so comfortable I could almost forgive the hideous pattern of ruby-red flowers that covered them like a rash. Almost.

After a quick tour of the place, and an attempted phone call home, Marion had left me 'to get settled in'. There had been no answer from home, and I found it strange that neither Mum nor Ameena were in. No doubt I was being paranoid and there was a simple explanation for it – shopping, or something. I made a mental note to call again later.

The room Marion had picked for me looked out on to the wooded hillside that led up from one side of the house. At the top of the hill, a towering metal structure rose above the treetops. It looked almost alien against its surroundings, and I guessed it must be a television or radio mast.

I could hear Marion bustling about in the kitchen making dinner. I'd never tasted her cooking, but statistically it was very unlikely to be as bad as Mum's. I hadn't eaten anything since leaving home, and I realised I was actually quite hungry.

Marion had already made it clear dinner would be a good hour or so away. I sprung up from the bed. Even out here there had to be somewhere to buy snacks. Right?

'A shop? Yes, of course there's a local shop,' Marion told me. She stopped stirring the bubbling contents of a large metal pot for a moment, wiped her hands on her apron, and then pointed out through the open back door. 'You know the drive we came up?'

'Yep.'

'Head back down it until you reach the road, then turn left.'

'Left,' I nodded. 'OK.'

'Then you just keep walking straight on.'

'For how long?'

'About twenty-seven miles,' she said. 'It's on the right. You can't miss it.'

'*Twenty-seven miles?*' I groaned. 'Seriously?'

'Afraid so,' she said, returning to her stirring. 'Listen, dinner will be less than an hour. Why don't you go for a wander outside for a while? I'll give you a shout when it's ready. You could have a look for Toto for me. Just don't go too far from the house.'

I hesitated, considering just heading back up to my room and riding out the hunger pangs. A smell had begun to rise from the cooking pot, though, and it was making me feel even more ravenous. Maybe getting outside for a while was a good idea.

'Get a shift on then,' Marion urged, as she ground some pepper into the pot. 'Take the chance to get out and explore while you can.' She turned to me, unable to mask her mischievous grin. 'Because I've got a real treat in store for you after dinner.'

'Oh?' I asked, intrigued. 'What's that?'

'You're on dishes!'

The hillside was steep, but the tangle of thick roots that covered the ground acted almost like steps, making climbing easier. I had decided to check out the mast on the hilltop, but now I was actually in the forest, the trees blocked it from view. As a result, I had absolutely no idea if I was headed in even vaguely the right direction.

A high embankment rose up in front of me and I had to scramble on all fours to get to the top. I had only been walking for about five minutes, but already the terrain was taking my breath away, and not in an *Ooh, that's pretty* kind of way. I spent a few seconds resting against a tree, before continuing onwards and upwards.

Marion seemed nice, but already I could feel I was beginning to miss Mum. Some people might have found it strange that I'd never spent a night away from her before, but then it wasn't like I'd ever had a lot of places to go and stay.

I'd never had many friends, and the few I'd managed to make I didn't know well enough to sleep over at their houses. That left only family, and I didn't exactly have much of that, either.

My nan lived with us up until she'd gone into the care home, so staying at her place overnight had never exactly been an option. And then there was my dad. The less said about him, the better.

He was the one who sent Mr Mumbles and Caddie after me. He was the one to blame for everything that had happened over the past few weeks. And he was the reason I was here now, hiding in the middle of nowhere, a hundred miles from home. And the worst thing was, I didn't even know why he was doing it.

Thinking about my dad had got my blood pumping and my heart thudding against my chest. I'd spent the last few minutes powering up the hill, hauling myself along using low-hanging branches and trailing roots.

The further up the hillside I went, the denser the forest became. The treetops were so close together now I could barely make out the darkening sky. Dusk had been approaching when I left the house, but now night was fast drawing in.

I turned and looked back down the hill. A weak, watery light highlighted the details of the woods around me, but beyond that everything merged into murky shades of grey.

'Great,' I muttered, realising now why Marion had told me not to go too far from the house. Checking out the mast would have to wait.

I slowly began to pick my way back down, hesitating every few steps as I scanned for somewhere safe to place my feet. The roots that had been so helpful on the way up now seemed intent on catching on my toes or tangling around my ankles. They made progress slow, and the darkness tightened further around me with every step I took.

After several minutes of walking, I realised I should have come across the large embankment again. The fact that I hadn't was worrying. It meant I wasn't following the same route down as I had on the way up. I looked to the sky to try to find my bearings, but there was nothing in the gloom to show me the way.

I stumbled over a broken root and had to catch hold of a tree trunk to stop myself falling. I leaned against the tree, giving myself a few seconds to recover from the fright.

As I stood there, I heard something move in the darkness. At first it was almost nothing – a gentle rustling of leaves; the faint *crunch* of a footstep on rotten twigs. Quickly, though, it picked up in pace, rushing towards me through the undergrowth, closer and closer, faster and faster.

Whatever it was, I could hear its breathing now. Each panted breath sounded low and rasping and hoarse. I wasn't sure what would breathe quite like that, but I knew one thing for sure.

It wasn't anything human.

Chapter Seven

UNDER ATTACK

A dark grey shape about the size of a large cat bounded through a bush and stumbled to a stop a few metres away. It cocked its head quizzically to one side and looked up at me. I almost laughed with relief.

'Hey,' I said, taking a step closer to the animal, 'you must be Toto.'

The little terrier pulled back as I approached. A growl rumbled in the back of his throat. It sounded much deeper and more threatening than I expected from a dog that size.

'It's OK,' I said, keeping my voice light, 'I'm not going to hurt you.' I took another step towards him. He growled again, but it was a half-hearted effort this time, and I could tell it was all for show.

Two more steps and I was crouching down beside the dog. His fur felt matted and damp as I gently patted him. His little body was radiating heat, and I could feel his breath panting in and out.

'Been running, boy?' I said softly. He pulled back slightly at the sound of my voice, but otherwise didn't react.

I patted him a little more firmly, letting my hand travel across his head and down over his narrow back. As my hand brushed over the fur near his tail, he gave a sharp yelp and leapt backwards.

'What's the matter, Toto?' I asked. 'Are you...' In the pale light I saw the streak of blood on my hand. '...hurt?'

Toto let out another low growl. I began to say sorry for hurting him, before I realised he wasn't growling at me. His head was craned back, looking up into the trees. His eyes flicked erratically from treetop to treetop, as if searching for something.

I stood up and followed his gaze, but could see nothing through the gloom other than the occasional swaying branch. Toto's growling was becoming louder. His tail was between his legs, and the wiry hair on his back was pointing to the sky. Something was scaring him. Badly.

'It's OK, boy, there's nothing there,' I said. 'It's just the wind making the trees move, that's all. It's nothing to—'

A black shape swooped down from the treetops. I heard it first – a rustle in the darkness, followed by a faint *whoosh* as the bird flew past my head. I saw Toto spin on the spot, watched him bare his teeth. He snapped his tiny jaws around thin air, then yelped as the crow pecked sharply at his ear.

The whole attack lasted less than a second. The bird was back up in the trees before I could even react. I peered up into the branches, searching for any sign of it. It wasn't easy, but eventually I found it – a darker shade against the grey-black of the evening sky. It folded and unfolded its wings a few times as I watched, but otherwise didn't show any sign of moving.

I turned back to Toto, only to find him flat on his belly. His eyes were open, still staring up into the trees. He was shivering and whining softly, and I could see a deep cut in his ear where the bird had nipped at him.

'Don't worry, it's staying up there,' I said, glancing back to where I expected to see the bird. But instead of one black shape, I saw two. They sat together on a high limb, so close they were almost touching.

A movement in the branches above them caught my eye. Another crow sat there, glaring down. My eyes moved slowly across the canopy of treetops, finding more and more dark outlines perched on every branch. There were dozens of them, easily fifty or more. A few of them gave hoarse, croaky *caws* as my gaze swept over them.

'OK,' I muttered, steadying myself. 'It's nothing. They're just birds.'

I made a move towards Toto. A few of the crows hopped down on to lower branches. Their eyes shone against their masks of black feathers, flicking from me to the dog and back again.

I hesitated for a moment, watching the birds. They shuffled from foot to foot, but kept their wings folded against their backs. 'Just birds,' I repeated below my breath. I turned and took another step towards the terrified Toto.

As if on some secret signal, every one of the birds moved. They leaned forward on the branches and plunged towards the ground, flicking their wings wide at the last possible moment.

The air around me became thick with oily-black feathers. They beat against my cheeks and swished through my hair. Flashes of beaks and of eyes and of sharp, outstretched claws were all I could see. I ducked down, crossing my hands over my face to protect myself. Just a few metres away, I heard Toto break into a frenzied barking.

The sound seemed to draw the birds over. They left me and rounded on the little dog. They hovered around him like a thundercloud, blocking him from view, their throaty cries almost drowning out his barks.

For a few moments they flapped and fluttered wildly around him. Then, without warning, every bird dived at once, attacking in perfect formation. Toto squealed and yelped as the crows' beaks tore into his flesh.

A surge of electrical energy buzzed across my scalp, and I felt my power surge through my veins. I opened my mouth and a sound like thunder uttered its voice: 'Leave him alone!'

The tornado of beating wings suddenly swirled around me again. Birds thudded into my back, snapped at my face, dug their claws into my arms. Panic tightened my stomach and made my legs shake. The power crackled behind my eyes, but there were too many of them, flying too fast. I tried to focus, but I couldn't. I couldn't stop them. I couldn't fight back.

And then, moving as if it were a single creature, the flock banked up into the trees and vanished back among the branches. I braced myself for the expected pain, but it didn't come. Amazingly, other than a few scratches on my arms, I was unhurt. The crows may have attacked me, but they hadn't done any real damage.

The same couldn't be said for Toto.

Matted balls of bloodied hair lay dotted around the clearing. A slick sheen of red coated the forest floor. It made the ground slippery beneath my feet as I approached the ravaged remains of Marion's dog.

Bones stuck up at awkward angles from the little mound of flesh and fur. Toto's ribcage had been picked almost completely clean. It looked artificially white against the dark crimson of the animal's innards.

The stench was choking. It caught in the back of my throat and made me gag. My saliva turned sour in my mouth and I bent double, splattering the ground with what little there was in my stomach.

In the forest canopy above me, I heard the crows. They called to each other – or to me – a sinister *caw-caw-caw* that sounded almost like laughter. I looked for them, but the darkness was thicker than ever and I could barely see even the lower limbs of the trees. If I was ever going to find my way back to the house, I had to get moving.

I glanced briefly at what had once been Toto, whispered an apologetic goodbye, then set off hurriedly down the hillside, watched all the way by a hundred black, soulless eyes.

* * *

'Ah, the wanderer returns!' laughed Marion, looking up from the newspaper she was reading at the small kitchen table. I smiled sheepishly, and closed the back door behind me. 'I'd started to think you weren't coming back,' she added.

'Sorry,' I told her. 'I started walking up to the big mast thing and… it got dark. I got a bit lost.'

She waved a hand as if dismissing the apology, got up from the table, and crossed to the cooker. 'Easily done,' she said. 'You haven't been that long. I've been keeping dinner warm.'

I stood there, just inside the doorway, shuffling uneasily from foot to foot and watching her turn up the heat on the stove.

'Did you make it? To the mast?' she asked.

'What? No. No, I didn't.'

'Good!' she said, giving her cooking pot a stir. 'Dangerous brute of a thing. Radioactive, they reckon.'

'Radioactive?'

'Something to do with the signals or something,' she

shrugged. She lifted the pot and spooned some of the contents on to two large plates. 'Don't know much about them myself, mobile phones. Maybe it's a load of rubbish about the radiation, but who knows? Keep clear, that's what I say. Better safe than sorry.'

'Oh, it's a mobile phone mast?' I asked, remembering the phone Mum had given me. I still needed to plug it in and charge it up.

'It is indeed. Went up about a year and a half ago. Big complaints about it. Lot of fuss.'

I watched her cross back to the table and put the plates on it. She sat on her chair and picked up a fork and knife. 'Well, come on then,' she urged. 'Before it gets cold.'

Marion had fetched another chair from somewhere and placed it across from hers. Its wooden legs squeaked on the floor when I pulled it out from below the table. I sat down and stared at my plate. Chunks of meat sat on it, still attached to spindly white bones. They were stacked up into a kind of pyramid, and surrounded by a dark liquid. Mushrooms, carrots and transparent slices of onion all added substance to the already thick gravy. It looked good. It smelled great.

But all it reminded me of was Toto.

'It's lamb casserole,' Marion explained, noticing my hesitation. 'I use lamb chops on the bone. Adds to the flavour.'

I felt my mouth filling up with saliva again and had to swallow back another retch. Marion had one of the lamb chops in her hand, and was stripping it with her teeth. I looked away, but heard the meat tear as she bit down.

'Eat up,' she said, between mouthfuls. 'How do you expect to fight *him* if you don't keep your strength up?'

I looked across at her. 'Fight who?'

'This bully you told me about.'

'Bully?'

'The one you're hiding up here from.'

'Oh,' I said, remembering the lie, 'him.'

I picked up a fork and pronged a mushroom. It tasted good, but squelched unpleasantly as I chewed it. I got through it, though, and my hunger gradually took over from the sick feeling in my stomach. I picked my way through the veg, but couldn't face tackling the meat.

'Come across Toto when you were out?' asked Marion, as I skewered three chunks of carrot and a slice of onion.

'No,' I said, before quickly cramming the forkful into my mouth.

'Oh well, he'll turn up soon enough,' she smiled, although I could see she was concerned. 'When he's hungry, most probably.'

I nodded, but didn't say anything. I should have told her what had happened the second I'd come through the door, but I couldn't bring myself to do it. I hadn't known her long, but I was sure she would be heartbroken about the dog. From what I could tell he was her only real companion out here. With him gone she would be utterly alone.

'He knows where he's got it easy,' Marion continued. 'Never stays away for long. It's like they say in the film, I suppose. "There's no place like home".'

'What film?' I asked.

Marion leaned back in her chair a little and blinked

several times rapidly. 'You mean you don't know?'

I shook my head. 'Should I?'

'It's *The Wizard of Oz*, of course!'

'Oh,' I said. 'Never seen it.'

'What, *never*?'

I shrugged. 'Don't think so.'

Marion looked shocked, but excited at the same time, as if she'd just won the lottery without even buying a ticket. She got up from the table, scraped the remains of her dinner into a little red dog bowl, then placed her plate in the sink. When she turned back to me, a broad smile was spread across her face.

'When you're finished come through to the living room,' she said. 'Do I have a treat in store for you!'

The old VCR gave a *whirr* and a *clunk* when Marion stopped the tape. She adjusted herself in her armchair so she was facing across to the couch where I was sitting, enjoying the warmth of the fire burning in the hearth.

'Well?' she breathed. 'What did you think?'

'It was all right,' I said, as enthusiastically as I could manage.

'All right?'

'No, I mean, it was good, yeah.'

'Who was your favourite character?' she asked, her eyes sparkling even more than usual.

I paused for a moment, trying to remember anything of what I'd just seen. Marion had been really excited about showing me the film, but I found it a bit boring. I also had the all-too-vivid memories of a dead fat man and a dead dog gnawing away at my brain, so I hadn't really been paying all that much attention.

'The flying monkey guys were quite cool,' I said, recalling one of the few moments I'd actually been following what was happening on the small television screen.

Marion rolled her eyes and chuckled. 'Might have known you'd go for them,' she said. 'Typical boy. I like Scarecrow, myself. I still hide behind the cushion when I see him catch fire. Just can't bear to watch it.'

'I wondered why you were doing that,' I told her.

Marion got up from her chair and ejected the video. She carefully slipped it back into its faded case and returned it to a shelf above the old television. 'I must say, it's nice to have someone to watch it with,' she said. 'Toto just doesn't appreciate it at all.'

A flicker of concern crossed her face and she glanced towards the window. Like those in the kitchen, it had wooden shutters instead of curtains. They were open now, revealing nothing but darkness beyond the glass. 'I hope he's all right,' she said. 'He's never normally gone for this long.'

I gently cleared my throat. 'Marion,' I began. 'Toto's...'

When I didn't continue she said, 'Toto's what?'

'Probably just wandering,' I replied, faking a smile. 'He'll come back when he's hungry. You said so yourself.'

Her expression remained the same for a few seconds, before finally melting into a smile. 'He does like to go exploring,' she said. 'He'll come back when he's hungry.'

My lie of a smile stayed fixed on my face, but I couldn't

hold her gaze any longer. I turned away, searching for a way to change the subject.

'What's that?' I asked, spotting a large wooden box like a treasure chest over by the corner of the room.

'That, young man,' she said, her blue eyes shimmering with excitement, 'is my dressing-up box!'

I looked at her. 'You have a dressing-up box?'

'It's from when I was a girl,' she said, laughing. 'Of course I don't use it now.'

I pretended to wipe sweat from my brow. 'Phew.'

'Although,' she said, almost skipping over to the chest, 'what's say we have a little look inside?'

'Um, well, yeah, I suppose,' I said, 'but it's getting quite late.'

'Oh, come on, it's been years since I looked in here,' she said, taking hold of a handle on the side of the chest and dragging it into the middle of the room. 'A quick peek, that's all. What harm could it possibly do?'

Chapter Eight

DRESSING UP

I've never thought of myself as "cool". If anything, I'm the exact polar opposite of cool. I've been called a lot of names in school. Geek. Dweeb. Dork. Nerd. I've been called them all, mostly by the same three boys.

But not "cool". No one's ever called me that.

And there, kneeling on the floor beside a fifty-one-year-old woman as she rummaged around in a box full of fancy-dress outfits, I don't think I've ever felt more *uncool* in my life.

'Look at this! I'd forgotten about this one!' Marion chirped. She pulled out a crumpled pile of green material and looked at it as if it were carved from solid gold.

'What is it?' I asked, trying to get into the spirit of things, but failing miserably. It had been a long, horrible day and I'd barely slept the night before. I didn't want to look at costumes, I wanted to go to bed.

'It's a frog,' she said, with a tone that suggested I'd have to be an idiot not to realise what the scraps of cloth were meant to be. 'It's Mr Froggy.'

'So it is.'

Marion folded the costume neatly and sat it to one side. 'What else have we got in here?' she wondered, digging deeper down into the pile.

The frog outfit was the fourth one she'd pulled out. Or maybe it was the fifth. I couldn't say for sure. My ability to count had deserted me twenty minutes ago when she'd opened the chest. So had my will to live. This was torture.

'I used to fit in this fairy outfit,' she announced, holding up a pink leotard with cardboard wings attached. She was looking at the outfit, but her eyes seemed to stare through it. 'The fun I used to have,' she said quietly. 'Long time ago. Long time.'

It was one of those moments when I didn't know whether

to speak or not. She was lost in a memory, probably back as a fairy, dancing around this same house. I wondered how many years ago it had been.

'But listen to me,' she said, shoving the costume carelessly back into the trunk, 'rattling on about childish things.' She picked up some of the other outfits and began cramming them forcefully back inside the box. Her face was tinged with red, as if she was embarrassed at the way she had drifted off. 'You don't want to be sat here with me doing this. You'll be wanting your bed.'

I thought of the single chair beneath the kitchen table, and of the bowl of food set out for the dog that would never be coming home.

'It's fine,' I said. 'I'm enjoying it.'

She hesitated with a bundle of clothes halfway to the box. 'Really?'

'Yeah, it's good. It's interesting. Show me them all.'

'You sure?' Marion asked. 'There's quite a lot of them.'

I leaned over and peered inside the box properly. It was full to the top with the outfits. 'So there are,' I said, smiling too broadly. 'Must be fifty of them in there.'

'Probably more. You sure you want to see them all?'

I nodded, the plastic grin still stuck to my face. 'Yep,' I squeaked.

This was going to be a very long night.

'That's them all,' Marion said. Her head and shoulders were inside the costume chest, giving her voice a booming, echoing quality. 'Just odds and sods left.'

'Aww, that's a shame,' I said, fighting the urge to jump up and run around the room cheering.

'No, wait, I tell a lie. Here's one.'

I bit my fist. 'Yay!'

'Oh, now I remember this,' she said, holding up an orangey-brown jumpsuit with a furry hood. 'It's the lion.'

'It's a lion,' I agreed, trying to appear interested.

'No, it's *the* lion. The cowardly lion, from the film.'

'What film?'

She nudged me on the arm, almost making me topple over. 'Were you even watching it?' she asked. Her eyes were narrowed, but she was fighting back a smile. '*The Wizard of Oz.*'

'Oh, right, yes,' I stumbled. 'Um… I liked the flying monkeys.'

She rolled her eyes and chuckled. 'Boys!'

'Sorry,' I said, although I wasn't quite sure why.

She waved her hand, dismissing the apology. 'At least you pretended to watch it. That's good enough for me.' Her eyes went from the costume to me and back again. Finally she said, 'Actually, yes, you do owe me an apology. You need to make it up to me.'

I frowned. 'Um… what?'

'Put this on,' she said, passing me the lion outfit. 'See what it looks like.'

I stared down at the tatty orange bundle in my hands. It was made out of a stretchy material, like a thick pair of women's tights. 'You can't be serious.'

'Come on, it'll be fun,' she urged. Marion was keeping her face straight, but her eyes twinkled mischievously, like she could burst out laughing at any minute. 'Been forty years since I saw anyone wearing that outfit. Go put it on. Just for a minute.'

My mouth flapped open and closed as I searched for excuses. 'It'll be too small. It won't fit.'

'My friend used to wear it. He was about your size.'

'But it's... I mean, you can't... It's not...' Unable to find an end to any of those sentences, I decided just to surrender to my fate. 'OK,' I sighed, standing up. 'But only for a minute. And no laughing.'

Marion pretended to scratch her nose, but I could tell she was really just covering the smile that had spread across her face. 'Come on,' she said, her voice cracking. 'As if I would!'

Ten minutes later I stood outside the living room, adjusting the costume. Putting it on hadn't been the nicest experience. The whole thing smelled of damp and mould, and just as I'd expected, it was way too small. And because it was a one-piece outfit, this was causing me some problems.

For one thing, the sleeves were far too short, coming to

a stop halfway along my forearms, but that wasn't the big issue. The real problem lay in the legs.

The legs were exactly like tights in that they had feet at the bottom. This was fine – they stretched to allow my own feet in – but the legs were much shorter than my own. This meant that the crotch of the outfit hung down somewhere around my knees, and I'd had to contort my entire body to get the top part of the outfit up over my shoulders.

Now it was on, the stretched material was trying to snap back together. It pulled down on my shoulders, turning me into a sort of deformed hunchback figure. A deformed hunchback figure dressed as the lion from *The Wizard of Oz*.

Pulling the furry hood up over my head, I sighed and stepped into the living room. How the hell did I find myself in these situations?

'Ta-daa!' I said, holding out my arms as I entered the room, only to find nobody there. The costumes were still piled on the floor and the chest was still open, but there was no sign of Marion.

I returned to the hall, noticing how silent the house was.

Suddenly the forty-year-old fancy-dress costume I was wearing wasn't the only thing making me uncomfortable.

'Marion?' I said. No reply. I tried again, louder. 'Marion?' Again nothing.

Creeping across the hall I pushed open the door to the kitchen, half expecting to find a flock of birds in there. Instead I found an empty room, with the back door standing wide open.

'Marion, you there?' I called, edging towards the open door. Clouds of cold air rolled in through the gap, making me shake and shiver like... well, like a cowardly lion.

As I drew nearer the door I saw her. She was standing just outside the house, looking out into the darkness. A full bowl of dog food was clutched in her hands.

'There you are,' I said, stepping out to join her and immediately wishing I hadn't. The cold was biting and my current attire was hardly designed for warmth. 'You OK?'

'Still no sign of him,' she said. 'I'm really starting to get worried now.'

I didn't speak. I couldn't tell her the truth. Not now. Not after leaving it so long.

'He'll be fine.'

'I'm not so sure,' she said, pulling her cardigan tightly around her neck. 'It doesn't feel right. Something's wrong. Something's happened.'

She spent another few moments scanning the darkness, before finally turning to face me. Her expression went from sad to surprised to delighted in under a second.

'Oh my goodness. You look—'

'Like an idiot?'

'Well, it's not *quite* the word I'd have chosen,' she grinned. 'But maybe it *is* a little bit on the neat side. Joe couldn't have been as tall as you, after all.'

'Joe?' I asked, through chattering teeth.

'The old friend of mine I mentioned.' She gestured with the dog bowl towards the door. 'Now get inside before you freeze.'

I gratefully rushed back inside, not stopping until I was in the living room, where the fire crackling in the hearth quickly began to warm me up. Marion arrived a few moments after me, Toto's bowl no longer in her hands.

'Now,' she said, 'where's that camera?'

'Don't you dare!'

'Kidding,' she laughed. 'I think you've been tortured quite enough for one night.'

I smiled, relieved. 'Thanks.'

'Besides, you're here for ages yet. Plenty more costumes for you to try on.' She caught my expression and gave another laugh. 'I'm joking. You have to stop taking me so seriously.' Her eyes went to the stash of clothes on the floor as she remembered something. 'Although, come to think about it...'

I stood there by the fire, hunched over in my badly fitting lion costume, watching her rummage through the outfits. Silently, I gave thanks that Ameena wasn't around to pass comment.

'I've got Dorothy's dress and the Tin Man's hat,' Marion announced, holding up a blue and white checked outfit and a metal funnel. 'I'm sure I used to have the full set, but one's missing. That's a shame.' She held the items higher. 'Fancy either of these?'

'I'll pass, thanks,' I said.

She nodded and smiled. 'Fair enough.' Her bones creaked as she got to her feet. 'Now, it's high time you were in bed.'

I looked at the clock and was shocked to see the hands had crept past midnight. Too late to phone Mum now. 'Suppose so,' I agreed. I hovered awkwardly near the door for a few moments, then said, 'Night, then.'

'Goodnight, Kyle,' Marion said. 'And thank you.'

'What for?'

'For being good company. I haven't had such a laugh in a long time.'

'Oh,' I said. I didn't think I'd been *that* funny. 'No problem. I mean, good. I enjoyed it too,' I continued, and I wasn't lying.

Marion sat down in her armchair and gazed into the fire. I moved to leave, but hesitated again just inside the doorway. 'It must get lonely out here,' I said. 'All on your own.'

'Oh, don't worry about me, I'm not on my own,' she replied. 'I've got Toto.'

Ouch. I quickly changed tack. 'But, I mean, isn't there anyone else? What about your friend. Joe, did you say his name was? What happened to him?'

Marion adjusted herself in her chair. 'We... drifted apart. Haven't seen him in decades,' she said with a shrug. 'Still, these things happen. Friendships come and go.'

I gave another nod. I knew one or two things about broken friendships.

'I *was* lonely once upon a time, back when I was a girl. No other children for miles. Just my parents for company,' she said, her eyes taking on that faraway look again. 'And then *he* came along. I think I was five or six when he turned up, and suddenly... I wasn't lonely any more.

'He was older than me. A lot older, older than my father, even, but it didn't matter because in many ways he was just like a child. We'd go for walks in the woods. Play games. He loved dressing up. We both did. Disguising ourselves, pretending to be other people. It was exciting. In some ways I think he was only truly happy when he was being someone else.'

'Didn't your parents mind, though? You hanging about with a strange man like that?'

'Oh no, they didn't really mind,' she said with a chuckle. 'How could they? They never saw him. No one ever saw him but me.'

The lion costume seemed to become even tighter around me, squeezing the air from my insides. I shifted my weight on my feet, and realised my back was suddenly clammy with sweat.

'What do you mean,' I said hoarsely, *no one saw him but you?*'

Marion laughed. 'Makes me sound crazy, doesn't it?' She picked up a poker and jabbed it into the fire, sending sparks fluttering up the chimney. 'I called him Joe Crow,' she said, smiling wistfully. She looked up at me, and the words she spoke shook me to my core.

'He was my imaginary friend.'

Chapter Nine

RUDE AWAKENING

My heart missed a beat. I was on the move before it found the next one.

'The doors,' I said urgently. 'Lock the doors.'

Marion's smile faltered. 'What? Whatever for?'

I didn't dare take the time to explain. Instead I ran from the living room and into the kitchen, where I knew the back-door key was waiting in the lock. I turned it, checked the door was shut tight, and doubled back through to the other room.

Marion was still in the living room, but out of her seat and by the door. 'Kyle? What's the matter?'

'Are there shutters on all the windows?' I asked, slowing but not stopping as I made for the front hall.

'Most of them, yes, but what's—'

'Listen to me,' I said, locking my eyes on hers, 'I need you to close all the shutters on the downstairs windows, OK? I'll lock the front door and do the upstairs ones.' I pointed to the hot poker she still held in her hand. 'Keep that with you, and if you see anything moving, whack it until it stops.'

'What?' Marion spluttered. 'Don't be ridiculous. It might be Toto!'

'Trust me,' I mumbled, hurrying through to the hall, 'it won't be Toto.'

There was no key in the front-door lock. I glanced around in case it was hanging on a hook or something, but found nothing.

'Marion, where's the front-door key?' I shouted.

'I'm not sure,' she replied from right behind me. 'I don't really bother to lock it.'

'What are you doing?' I demanded, turning to face her. 'You need to go and close the shutters. Now!'

'But why, Kyle?' she asked, making no attempt to hide

the concern in her voice. 'What's the matter? What are you so afraid of?'

'I'll tell you later, I promise. But for now, we need to get the shutters closed and doors locked, OK?'

She hesitated, then gave a brief nod. 'All right. I'll get the shutters.' Her eyes darted to the door at my back. 'But I really don't know where the key is.'

'Don't worry, I'll sort it,' I told her. 'Now hurry. We might not have much time.'

The sparks were buzzing through my brain before she'd even left the hall. I had barely begun to picture the lock mechanism moving when it gave a solid *clunk*. Who needed keys when you had an imagination like mine?

I took the narrow stairs two at a time and rushed to the end of the top landing, where a wide window opened out over Marion's vegetable garden. The wooden shutters closed over easily, clipping in place with a small metal latch. As barricades went, they weren't the strongest, but they were all we had.

The window in my room had no shutters, so I pushed the

heavy oak wardrobe in front of the glass, then wedged the bottom of the bed against it, jamming the wardrobe in place.

There were no shutters in the bathroom, either, but the window was tiny, and I couldn't see anything dangerous fitting through. I was about to leave it uncovered when I remembered the window in the train toilet compartment. It was just as small as this one – maybe even smaller – but it had been big enough for something to come through and murder the man-baby.

Like a slap to the face, the realisation hit me. The window in the train was too small for a human to get through, but it was big enough for a crow. They'd been flying alongside the train, hadn't they? One must've come through the window and killed the man.

But why? What did he have to do with anything? What was I missing?

I gave myself a shake and focused on the problem at hand. The house had to be secured first. Everything else could wait.

There was a medicine cabinet mounted on the bathroom wall. I unhooked it and jammed it between the window and the metal taps of the sink. The base of the cabinet fitted quite tightly against the taps, so while it wouldn't put up a lot of resistance if something really wanted to get in, it wouldn't just fall off at the first push. It wasn't ideal, but it would have to do.

I rushed through the remaining two rooms – a makeshift study and Marion's pristinely neat bedroom – fastening the shutters in both. When I was satisfied that upstairs was as secure as I could make it, I wasted a few seconds getting out of the lion outfit and back into my own clothes, then I hurried down to join Marion.

I found her in the living room. She was standing by the shuttered window, holding the telephone to her ear. She gave me a worried smile as I entered the room.

'Who are you phoning?' I asked.

'Your mum,' she told me, sliding the handset back into its cradle. 'But there's no answer.'

I stopped, all thoughts of securing the building

temporarily forgotten. 'What, *still*? But it's late. She's never out late.'

'Maybe there's a problem with the phone line or something. It happens.' Marion sat in her armchair and gazed up at me. The flames in the fireplace threw long shadows across her face. 'Now,' she said, 'why don't you tell me what all this is about?'

Half a dozen plausible lies popped into my head. It was hard to choose one, so in the end I didn't. I sat on the couch, gazed into the fire, and quietly told her the truth.

A few hours later, I lay in bed, not quite asleep and not fully awake, listening for anything that sounded like trouble. So far I'd heard nothing unusual, but if Marion's "Joe Crow" had come back, it was surely only a matter of time before he put in an appearance.

The conversation with Marion had gone about as well as expected. Very badly. She'd been nice enough about it all, nodding when she was supposed to, frowning on cue. But it was an act, I knew. No matter how much she tried to pretend otherwise, she hadn't believed a word.

And who could really blame her? There I was, a relative stranger, telling her that not only did I see imaginary friends, but that they kept trying to kill me. Did I honestly expect her to believe any of it?

The fact was, I *didn't* expect her to believe me, but I didn't want to lie to her. I'd lied to her already about Toto, and that was bad enough. Even when she'd thought I was a criminal she had let me into her house. She'd been willing to protect me, and if I'd brought danger to her doorstep, I was going to do everything I could to protect her. Even if it did make her think I was crazy.

I'd tried phoning Mum again – partly so she could back up my story, but mostly to set my own mind at rest. She didn't answer. Nobody answered, not even when I let the phone ring for over five minutes. Marion tried to reassure me, but the way the hairs on the back of my neck stood up told me something was wrong. I made up my mind then that I would be on the first train home in the morning.

The lights were off inside the house, and the wardrobe

kept all but the faintest glimmers of moonlight out. I lay there with only the glow from the bedside radio alarm clock for company, willing the dawn to come. Marion had given me a candle and a battered old metal lighter. I'd sat the candle on the bedside table, but made sure the lighter stayed in my jeans pocket on the other side of the room, just in case I was tempted to use it. Light – even a weak one – might attract something, and that was the last thing I wanted to do.

My mobile phone was also on the bedside table, charging up so I could keep trying to get through to Mum during the journey home. It *was* possible there was a fault with the phone line, but I doubted it. It was too much of a coincidence. Something was definitely wrong, and the sooner I could find out what, the better.

It was the warbling of a woman's voice that woke me up. Her high, operatic soprano squawked sharply from the radio alarm, jolting me upright in the bed.

The dim glow of the morning sunlight squeezed through

the narrow gaps around the wardrobe and into the room. I was so tired my eyes felt like shrivelled holes in my face, and I had to blink half a dozen times just to bring the bedroom into focus.

When I could see properly, I checked the clock. It was a few minutes past eight – much later than I had planned to sleep. I took my mobile from the bedside table. It gave a faint *bleep* as I switched it on.

Even before the phone had finished starting up, I heard the scratching. Instinctively, my eyes went to the ceiling. Mr Mumbles had first shown up in my attic, making his presence known by scraping on the floor, which was directly above my room.

As this scratching continued, though, I realised I was looking in the wrong place. The noise wasn't coming from above me this time.

It was coming from below.

I lay there and listened, trying to ignore the radio so I could focus on the sound beneath the bed. I've never liked opera music, but playing it on the radio at eight in the morning should be against the law, especially as the urgency of the woman's voice was making me even more nervous than I already was.

As I listened, I realised it wasn't just a scratching beneath my bed. There was another sound too – the occasional soft *thud* of something hitting the wooden floorboards.

Cautiously, I edged my head down over the side of the bed. The space beneath it was filled with shadow, and at first I couldn't see anything. The daylight coming in through the ajar bedroom door took the edge off the darkness, though, and it took my eyes just a few seconds to adjust.

The woman on the radio hit a high note just as I spotted the crow. It was crouching beneath the bed, shuffling awkwardly from side to side. It didn't seem to notice me as it pecked at a little white ball it had found. Every time it pecked at the ball it would flick it a few centimetres into the air, before catching it in its beak and letting it fall back to the floor with a *thud*.

I slowly pulled myself back up into bed, being careful

not to make any sound. The crow was big, just like the ones that had descended on Toto the day before. I leaned back against my pillows and tried to figure out the best thing to do.

Creak. The springs of the mattress groaned as my weight shifted. With a strangled screech, the crow exploded from beneath the bed. The bird rose quickly, flipped in the air, and pulled off an incredibly tight turn. Its eyes shone like black gemstones as it banked and dived straight towards my face.

I threw the covers up above my head, just as the crow hit my pillow. I heard its claws tear through the fabric, felt its beak pecking furiously at the top of the blanket.

Scrambling down the bed, I wriggled out through the feet-end of the covers, close to where the bed frame was wedged against the wardrobe. The bird looked up at me and gave an angry *caw*. Before it could attack, I caught the bottom of the blankets and flipped them over the crow. Leaping back on to the bed, I pinned the covers down, trapping the bird beneath them.

For a few long moments there was no sound in the room but my breathing and the drone of the opera on the radio. The only movement was the heaving of my chest. Beneath the blanket, everything was still.

I cautiously lowered my head towards the covers, turning my ear as I tried to listen for anything that would tell me what the bird was doing. The blankets were thick, and the space beneath them tight. With any luck the crow had suffocated already.

Nothing. The bird seemed silent and still. I inched my ear a little closer, trying to tell for sure if—

The beak tore through the blanket with a single peck. I felt a flash of pain and my hand flew to my ear. When I pulled it away, my fingers were wet with my blood.

The crow's head was squirming through the hole in the covers, each wriggle forcing the tear wider. I leapt backwards off the bed, releasing my pin-hold on the blankets.

Those beady black eyes stayed fixed on me as the bird fought to free itself. I felt the electrical tingle on my scalp, but I was too panicked to know what to do with it. My abilities relied on me using my imagination, and right now my imagination couldn't come up with anything that could deal with a flesh-eating crow.

Before I could think of something, the bird tore free. It beat its oily wings until it was up near the ceiling. Then, with a demonic screech, it swooped towards me.

The next few seconds became a blur as several things happened at once.

The warbling of the woman on the radio became distorted by the buzzing of some sort of interference. Even as the interference began, the crow was veering wildly off course. It thudded headfirst against the wall just as my mobile phone began to ring. I heard the bird's neck snap, and knew it was dead before it hit the floor.

I was too shocked to move at first. Quickly, though, I made a dive for the phone, frantically searching for the button to answer it.

'You have four new voicemail messages,' a robotic voice informed me. 'First new message...'

There was a brief pause before Ameena's voice broke in.

'Kyle, it's me. Listen, if you get this, you have to come back. Now. It's your mum,' the recording said, and I felt my pulse quicken. 'On the way back from the station, she was... We were attacked. I tried to stop him, but he was too big, I...' Her voice was becoming more panicked. She cleared her throat and when she spoke again she sounded a little less frantic. 'Listen, just come back when you get this, OK?'

The line gave a *bleep* and the next message began.

'Me again,' Ameena said. 'I'm at the hospital. Where are you?'

Bleep.

'What's the point in even having a phone if you don't switch it on?' Ameena spat. She was breathless, as if she was running while she was talking. 'I've just left the hospital. The doctors say your mum's stable for now. I'm going back to the house to get the address you're at, then I'm coming to find you, so stay put. If the guy who attacked your mum comes for you, I don't like your chances on your own.

'Keep your eyes open for him,' she continued. 'He's a big fat guy. Fattest guy I've ever seen. If you see him, run. I've seen what he can do, and it... Well, just run, OK? See you soon.'

Bleep.

'Nearly forgot to mention,' continued the next recording, 'so you'll know who to watch out for, he's bald too.

'And he really, really *stinks* of sour milk.'

Chapter Ten

SHEDDING SKIN

I tried calling home, but there was no answer. Not that I was surprised.

I didn't even stop to turn off the radio, or to do anything with the dead crow on the bedroom floor. Still clutching the phone in my hand I bounded down the stairs, calling out Marion's name as I ran.

She was standing in the kitchen, looking down at her hands as she flexed and unflexed her fingers over and over again. I could smell bacon and hear the sizzling of a frying pan on the stove behind her. A white surgical patch was taped over her right eye. The other seemed to sparkle an even brighter shade of blue, as if working to compensate.

It took a moment for me to realise, but Marion had

opened the shutters on the windows. The back door stood ajar too. Anything could have been let inside the house.

'Marion, you OK?' I asked, taken aback by her appearance. 'What happened?'

She brought up her head and lowered her hands. 'What? Oh, the patch. Pan spat oil at me. Stung a bit, that's all.' She glanced at the phone in my hand. 'Everything OK?'

'My mum's been attacked,' I said. 'She's in hospital.'

Marion's hand covered her mouth. 'Oh my God,' she muttered. 'Oh my God. Is she... I mean...'

'I don't know,' I told her. 'Can you take me to the train station? I know the windscreen's broken, but—'

'Of course I will,' Marion said. She looked me up and down. 'Better go get dressed first, though.'

I realised I was still wearing my pyjamas. 'Back in a minute,' I shouted over my shoulder, as I turned and rushed up the stairs to the bedroom. Something seemed off about Marion, but I guessed she was just worried about Toto. I should've told her the truth.

Still, there was no time now. Mum needed me. Nothing

else mattered but that.

I charged into the room and snatched up the clothes I'd been wearing the day before, not wanting to waste time unpacking clean ones. As I got dressed, I thought about Ameena's messages.

The man who had attacked them had to be the man from the train. How many fat bald men who smelled of milk could there be? He'd joined the train one stop after me, which meant he must've been able to move much faster than his size suggested.

Was *he* Marion's imaginary friend? Marion had said he was smaller than me, but then the Darkest Corners changed people, so that didn't rule him out. But he'd finished up as a wobbly pile of dead skin on the bathroom floor, so that probably *did* rule him out. If he was the one controlling the birds, why had they killed him?

I buttoned my jeans, pulled on my socks and looked around for my trainers. I could see one over by the door, but there was no sign of the other one anywhere.

I dropped to my knees and put my face close to the floor.

The shoe wasn't beneath the old chest of drawers, the bedside cabinet, or the wardrobe. Thrusting an arm below the bed, I felt around for the missing trainer. For a moment or two my fingers just trailed through dust, before finally brushing against something vaguely solid.

It took a second for me to realise what I'd found. I'd completely forgotten about the ball the crow had been tossing around. It felt soft and a little sticky in my hand. There was something attached to the top of it, like a short length of cord, or a piece of damp string.

Despite my hurry to get back to Mum, curiosity got the better of me. I pulled the thing out to take a proper look.

When I saw what I was holding, my hand spasmed, as if I had been electrocuted. The 'ball' gave a squelchy thud as it landed on the bare wooden floorboards.

On trembling legs I leapt up and backed away, fighting a rising feeling of sickness in my gut. I rubbed my hand against the front of my jeans, desperately trying to wipe off the thin layer of stickiness that clung to my palm.

Even as I did these things, the horror of what I was

looking at had only begun to filter through. Despite the urge to look away, I stared down at the squidgy round object, and it stared right back, lifeless and unblinking. An eyeball.

An eyeball with a piercing blue iris.

'M-Marion?' I could hear the shake in my voice when I called her name from the top of the stairs. Only the faint sizzle of frying bacon, and the persistent howling of the opera singer on the radio answered me back. 'Marion? You there?'

The top step gave a groan as I put my weight on it. I was about to continue down when I noticed the door to Marion's bedroom. It had swung half open, revealing her dressing table and part of one wall. Last night, when I'd gone in to lock the shutters, Marion's room had looked immaculate. Now the jars of creams and ointments that had stood neatly on the dressing table were scattered and toppled on the floor.

The step creaked again as I slowly back-paced to the top of the stairs. I'd found the missing shoe just outside the bedroom door and had quickly slipped it on. Even with my trainers' soft rubber soles, though, my steps echoed on the wooden floor. They resounded around the whole house as I crossed to Marion's room and edged in through the half-open door. I stopped just inside, my legs suddenly unwilling to take me any further.

The room was a mess, but I couldn't see it. The shutters were broken, the windowpane smashed, but I noticed neither one. All I could see – all that was in the room – was the *thing* on the bed.

It looked like Toto had, only much larger; a tangled mess of bones and flesh and black, oily feathers. A skeletal arm hung down over the ragged remains of the bedcovers. I watched, hypnotised by the steady *drip-drip-drip* of blood trickling from the fingertips.

I may have been there, but I felt strangely detached from it all, like an observer watching a recording of events years later. Maybe if the bits on the bed had looked more like a person I might have reacted differently. I might have *felt* differently. But the arm was the only thing to suggest I was looking at human remains. I kept my eyes fixed on it, followed every droplet of crimson as it meandered down the fingers and fell in slow motion to the floor. Focusing on the fingertips meant not focusing on anything else. Anything *worse*.

How long did I stand there? I honestly can't say. Time and the world beyond the room became meaningless, as if nothing existed but that place and that moment. All I know is that it was a while before the numbness became confusion, and a while later still when confusion was joined by the urgent gnawing of fear.

I didn't want to believe it was Marion, but who else could it be? There was no way to tell by looking at the remains, but I *knew* it was her. I'd have bet my life on it.

My lungs began to cramp up and I realised the rank smell of death had forced me to stop breathing. The walls around me seemed suddenly to bulge forward, closing in on me, squeezing out any clean air that was left in the room.

I had to get out. Had to get away from the room, away from the walls and the stench and the *thing* on the bed.

Chest burning, I spun round, ready to run from this place and never look back.

And then, there she was in the doorway. Large as life. Marion.

'Boo!' she said, and her lips drew sharply upwards into an impossible grin. Her whole face seemed to stretch, until I was sure that smile was going to tear her head wide open.

With a sudden jerk of her arm she tore the square of bandage from her eye. I caught a glimpse of empty darkness, before she doubled over, clutching at her sides and howling with laughter.

'M-Marion?'

Still laughing, she straightened and held her hands up for me to see. The ends of her fingers bulged grotesquely. I watched, too stunned to move, as one by one the fingertips split in half. From within the blistered skin other fingers emerged – longer and thinner, tapering into black, claw-like nails.

Marion's single eye was bulging from her face, swelling

to the size of a golf ball. When it finally popped from its socket she laughed harder than ever. It was a hissing, high-pitched giggle – loud enough to shake the remaining shards of glass from the window frame. I heard them shatter on the floor behind me as Marion dug her nails into her neck and began to pull.

She was still smiling as the skin across her throat split and her face slid backwards over her head. With a *schhlp* the mask of skin was pulled off, revealing another face underneath.

The face – the whole head – was made up of a rough brown sack, tied off at the neck. Its eyes were two dark, narrow holes. A wide mouth crammed with brown, rotting teeth took up the bottom half of the head. It wore Marion's grin like a trophy.

Stray strands of soiled straw poked out from where the head met the neck. The body that wriggled free of Marion's skin was agonisingly thin – barely half as wide across the shoulders as me. Its limbs were skinnier still, and far too long to be in proportion. Fully extended, they stretched down past the figure's knees, each one well over a metre from shoulder to claw.

The thing had no skin of its own. A red-and-white striped T-shirt and a pair of ragged dungarees covered most of its body, but those parts I could see were formed from decaying knots of straw and grass.

'A scarecrow,' I muttered in horror. 'Of course she'd have a scarecrow.'

With a final shuffle, he pulled his dirty work-boots clear of his disguise. Marion's blubbery skin lay in a heap by his feet. The spaces where her eyes had been stared blankly upwards, as if seeking mercy from some higher power.

That was the split second that everything fitted together. It wasn't a slow, dawning realisation, but a sudden jolt, as if someone had crept up and shouted the answer into my ear.

I'd been looking at it all from the wrong angle. A crow hadn't come in through the train window. Nothing had come in.

But something had gone out.

Joseph had told me to ask myself if the man had died before going into the bathroom or after. The question had seemed ridiculous at the time, and of course I'd said 'after'.

But I was wrong.

'*You*,' I croaked, 'it was you. On the train.'

The scarecrow's bulging head bobbed up and down like a novelty nodding-dog's. His straw hands made almost no sound as he clapped them enthusiastically together.

'You killed that man and… and…' I could barely bring myself to say it. 'And *wore him*. And Marion. You did the same to Marion.'

'What can I say, boy?' he sniggered. 'I just couldn't resist dropping in to meet you in person.' His voice was high and shrill, like metal rubbing on metal. Reaching into the chest pocket of his dungarees, he pulled out a crooked, mouldy carrot. The vegetable made an almost comical *boing* sound as he attached it to the middle of his face, just above his mouth. 'I'm a sucker when it comes to fancy dress!'

'And my mum. You hurt my mum!'

'Wrong! I *killed* her. I killed yo' momma dead,' he cackled. With a *whoop* of delight, he began to dance on the spot, singing: 'Ding dong, the witch is dead!'

'No, you didn't!' I bit back, and then immediately wished that I hadn't. He stopped dancing and stroked the bulge where his chin should have been.

'Well, ain't that a shame?' he muttered. 'Guess that's what happens when you go running off to catch a train.' He shrugged his pointed shoulders. 'Maybe I'll drop by and see her when I'm done with you. I reckon she'd like that, don't you, boy?'

It erupted like a volcano inside me. The thought of this... this *animal* being anywhere near my mum shocked my abilities into overload. I couldn't just feel the energy sparks this time, I could *see* them. They flooded out from within me until they covered every surface of the room like a living skin of electric blue.

A jagged triangle of glass rose from the floor behind me. Even without looking I could see it. I could see *everything* – every groove of the floorboards, every fibre of the wallpaper, every bloody scrap of Marion's remains. I could see it all, but all I focused on was the scarecrow.

And the broken glass.

With barely a thought, I sent the shard slicing past me. I felt the wind as it whipped past my cheek. Heard the *thup* as it found its target. The scarecrow was sent staggering backwards as the glass embedded itself deep into his chest.

Without moving, I reached out for more glass. Three deadly slivers rose into the air, rotating until their most pointed edges were aiming directly for the monstrosity in front of me.

Thwip. Another piece of the broken pane swished through the air at my command. It dug into his arm, just above the elbow.

Thwip. I sent another flying in his direction. This one was driven into his stomach. He stumbled backwards as I twisted the shard deeper inside him, making a tunnel all the way through to his back.

He was looking straight into my eyes when the final

shard hit him. It was the largest piece of all, with a wide, serrated edge that caught him across the throat and ripped clean through his neck. I didn't feel even an ounce of guilt, as I watched his head roll backwards and thud down on to the floor.

His body remained half upright, his back wedged against the wall of the upstairs hallway. The long, branch-like arms hung limply, his fingers almost touching the wooden floorboards.

Gradually, my rage faded, taking the shimmering glow that had covered everything with it. The numbness I had felt earlier began to creep back in, joined this time by a trembling that started at my feet and worked its way up until my whole body was shaking. I stared down at the expressionless face, barely able to believe what I'd just done.

Had I meant to kill him? I wasn't even sure. I'd wanted to stop him going after Mum, yes, and I wanted him to pay for what he'd done to Marion, but what I'd done went far beyond that. Something savage had assumed control, forcing me to finish him. To *murder* him in cold blood.

My abilities had almost taken over completely when I was fighting Caddie, and now it had happened again. It was as if they were feeding off my rage, growing stronger as my anger increased, turning me into a... a *monster*.

Just like my dad had told me they would.

I didn't flinch when the body slid sideways towards the floor, assuming it was just gravity at work. It wasn't until the arms began to move and the hands snatched up the fallen head that I realised something was very wrong.

The wide mouth was twisted into the now-familiar grin as the arms held the head in place above the stump of the scarecrow's neck. The severed strands of straw began to wriggle around like skinny worms. It took just seconds for them to start knotting together. A few moments after that and you'd never have known the head had ever been removed.

'Thought you had me there, didn't you, boy?' the scarecrow giggled. He idly plucked the shards of glass from his body and let them fall to the floor with a *chink*. His 'wounds' knitted closed immediately.

'If you reckon a little thing like that's gonna stop me, you ain't got no idea who you're dealing with,' he warned.

'I-I do,' I told him, rocked by what I'd just seen, but trying not to show it. 'I know who you are. You're Joe Crow.'

'Wrong again, boy,' he said, holding his scrawny arms above his head. 'They call me the Crowmaster!' The empty hollows that were his eyes turned towards the broken window.

'And here come my babies,' he said proudly. 'Don't you go running, now. I know for a fact they's all *dying* to eat you.'

Chapter Eleven

THROUGH THE SQUARE WINDOW

The Crowmaster moved faster than I've ever seen anything move before. He'd barely finished speaking when he took a sudden hop towards me, raising one knee to the level of his chest.

WHUMP! The sole of his boot crunched against my face, snapping my head back and driving me further into the bedroom. The pain came rushing in – a hot, firey ache that spread out from my nose and stabbed up into my brain.

The world around me went soft and wispy, like the inside of a cloud. Sounds became muffled and indistinct – the cawing of the crows; the giggle of the scarecrow hissing through his broken teeth; the pitter-patter of my blood as it flowed from my burst nose and dribbled to the floor.

I didn't feel myself fall. It wasn't until the rough hands caught me by the hair and dragged me towards the window that I realised I was on my knees. Fragments of glass tore into my legs as he pulled me across the floor. I kicked out, trying to stand up, but the one time I came close he knocked my legs from under me, forcing me back down.

'Word is you's somethin' special, boy,' he drawled, lifting me so my head was level with what was left of the window. He spat a thick wad of sticky black phlegm on to the floor by his feet. 'Don't look so special to me.'

Fighting through the pain, I concentrated on making the sparks come. It seemed to take longer than usual, but eventually I felt them pulsing through me, uncoiling their muscles and giving me strength. He wanted to see special? I'd show him—

KRAAK! He drove my head hard against the wooden windowsill. Another burst of agony exploded at my temple.

The sparks fragmented and shot off in every direction, like startled fish in a shallow pool. I tried, but unconsciousness was closing in too quickly for me to bring them back.

I felt his spindly fingers tightening around my throat. In one movement, he lifted me clean off the ground, shaking me like a rag doll until I forced my eyes to open.

'Not so fast there, boy. Don't want you passing out on me or nothin'. Reckon I wants you alive when them babies of mine rip your eyes clean from your head.'

He pulled me in close enough that I could smell the damp and decay on his breath. Maggots squirmed in the hollow of one of his eyes, gnawing hungrily on the rotting cloth that covered his head. His blackened teeth jutted up like crumbling headstones in the graveyard of his mouth. There was no part of his face that wasn't repulsive, but I couldn't bring myself to look away.

'Funny thing is, I ain't supposed to kill you. I'm just supposed to hurt you. Scare you. Do whatever I gotta, to make you do them special tricks of yours.

'Y'see, boy, he reckons that every time you do them

special tricks, the closer this here world of yours comes to disaster.' I felt his breath and spittle on my face as he yanked me even nearer to him. 'There's a gateway between your world and ours, he says, like a great big barn door, all locked up tight. And he reckons you the only one with the keys to unlock it.'

'Wh-who does?'

'Don't tell me you don't know, boy! Your daddy,' he said. 'Your daddy reckons you going to be the one to throw open them doors and let all us monsters loose.'

'He's wrong,' I slurred, pushing open my eyes. The world swam, never quite finding focus. 'It won't happen.'

'Oh, I know it won't happen, boy,' the Crowmaster nodded. 'It won't happen 'cos I ain't gonna let it.' He caught the confusion on my face and that laughter hissed out from within him again. *SS-SS-SS-SS.* 'Y'see, I got to thinking. I got to thinking, why share this place with anyone?

'I been stuck back in that hell-hole for nigh-on fifty years. Fifty years of being hunted and tortured by all them ugly freaks. Fifty years of scrabbling about in the dirt and the filth, like a hog. Fifty years of having to fight and kill every damn day just to stay living. Fifty. Long. Years.' He stabbed a finger towards the skeleton on the bed. 'Because of *that*. Because of *her*.'

'But... she didn't forget you,' I wheezed. My forgetting Mr Mumbles was what sent him to the Darkest Corners, but Marion had been talking about her imaginary friend just the night before.

Flecks of foam were forming around the scarecrow's mouth as he ranted. 'But she *outgrew* me. She didn't need me no more, so I ended up stuck in there with all them *things*.' He shook his head and spat on the floor again. I was no longer sure if he was even talking to me. 'And what, he wants me to bring all that here? He wants me to go back to living like that? Like an animal? It ain't gonna happen. This here world is gonna be mine. Mine and my babies'. Ain't no one else gonna share it.'

'S-so... you're going to let me go?' I asked.

His whole body was racked by his sickening laugh. 'You

soft in the head, boy?' he said. One of his long, pointed fingers jabbed me in the chest. 'Ain't you been listenin'? I'm gonna kill you.'

He pushed me towards the window. I fought against his grip, but it was too tight. I hammered his arms and kicked at his chest, but he was too strong. I screamed at him – pleaded with him – to stop, to let me go. But he didn't listen.

The January wind howled at my back, forcing its way up inside my T-shirt like an icy-cold hand. From the corner of my eye I could make out the ground. It looked hard and solid, and a long way away.

I screwed my eyes shut and concentrated, frantically trying to bring my abilities under control. But the wind, the pain, the scarecrow's rasping laughter – they all made it impossible to focus.

I was bigger than the window frame, but that didn't matter. In one shove he drove me through the old wood. I felt it splinter and snap; heard the final shards of the glass shatter and crack. And then there was nothing.

Nothing but the birds.

They flocked around me as I fell, swooping and diving, their sharp claws and beaks shredding through my clothes and ripping at my skin. Through the fog of screeching black I saw the Crowmaster. He was perched on the windowsill, laughing and pointing as I plunged backwards towards the ground.

Although it must've been over in seconds, that moment seemed to last for ever. The pain. The fear. And then, the desperate flicker of hope as I felt a faint surge of power buzz through my skull. It all seemed to happen at quarter-speed, right up until the moment I hit the ground.

WHUMPF. I bounced awkwardly off something soft, tumbled sideways in the air, then face-planted into the soil of Marion's vegetable plot. The crows' attack eased off, although I guessed they were just repositioning themselves for a fresh assault. Whatever, it gave me enough time to raise my head and look at what I'd crashed down on to.

A mattress lay beside me. It looked brand new – aside from a dark red streak where my blood had sprayed across it during the fall. It was thick and it was soft – soft enough to have saved my life.

And, without even thinking about it, I'd made it appear out of thin air. Despite everything that was happening around me, for a split second I just stared at the mattress. Had I created it? Or did someone somewhere suddenly have *their* mattress vanish out from underneath them? I thought again about Mr Mumbles and Caddie reappearing at my house. If I *had* somehow made the mattress, then maybe my theory was right. Maybe my imagination had brought both of them to life too.

A shadow grew larger around me, snapping me back to the present. I flopped on to my back just as the Crowmaster's boots crunched into the soil on either side of my head. From down on the ground he loomed like a giant; an unstoppable colossus, about to squash me underfoot.

'Well lookee-loo at you, boy,' the scarecrow spat. 'Maybe you's special after all.' He took a few steps back and raised his skinny arms. The crows flew into formation above him. They circled round and round just over his head, flying faster and faster until they were a tornado of spinning black. 'You scared of me, boy?' he demanded.

I shook my head. I was terrified, of course, but I wasn't about to give him the satisfaction of knowing.

The grin on his face said he knew I was lying. 'They are,' he said. 'My babies here, they's afraid of me. They's terrified, the lot of them. They's so terrified they'll do whatever I tell them to do.' He gave another hiss of laughter. 'Watch.'

The birds broke formation and flung themselves towards me. I curled my arms over my head. If I could protect myself for long enough, there was a chance – a slim one – that I could find a way out of this. The last thing I saw before I shut my eyes was a flash of open beak, and the jagged curve of an outstretched claw.

And then came an unexpected sound. The Crowmaster let out a roar – a furious shriek that echoed all the way from the house up to the forest, and back again.

I peeked through a gap in my arms and realised the birds were no longer moving to attack. They banked left and right, spinning and tumbling as they struggled to avoid crashing into one another. A few of them couldn't pull out fast enough, and collided clumsily in mid-air. Others thudded into the wall, flapped up on to the roof, or simply dropped like stones to the ground.

The Crowmaster stumbled through it all, his long arms waving around. He shouted and screeched and gnashed his rotten teeth, but his control over the birds had been broken by... something. But what?

It was then that my phone rang. I felt it at first – a sudden vibration in my jeans pocket that caught me by surprise and almost scared the hell out of me. A second later, the ringtone kicked in, shrill and tuneless, like the chorus of the crows themselves.

The ringing whipped the birds into even more of a frenzy. Their movements were panicked and erratic. Most of them were fleeing, while those that remained were either flapping around on the ground, or fighting among themselves.

Even the Crowmaster was affected by whatever had

startled the birds. He staggered unsteadily on his feet and flailed wildly with his arms, as if feeling his way through darkness.

Through it all, my phone kept ringing.

My brain still felt like it was floating in soup, but as I watched him claw at thin air, something went *click*. The holes in his head were just that – empty spaces, serving no purpose whatsoever. He had no eyes of his own, so he relied on the eyes of others. The eyes of his birds.

'I don't know how you did that, boy, but I ain't gonna let you do it again,' the scarecrow seethed. 'When I find you, I'm gonna hurt you. I'm gonna hurt you so bad you'll beg me to slit your throat an' be done with it.'

He stopped moving for a moment and seemed to find his bearings. With two strides of his stick-thin legs he reached me. A boot crumpled into my stomach, rolling me over on to my back. He bent at the waist, until his face was hanging directly above mine.

'Maybe I can't see you right now, but that ringer in your

pocket's making enough racket that I can still find you just the same.'

He brought his right hand down and felt through my hair, then down over my forehead until he reached my eyebrows. He flicked out his middle and index fingers and pressed the blackened nails against my cheeks until I gasped with the pain.

Through it all, my phone kept ringing.

'Maybe you stopped my babies taking your eyes, but you ain't gonna stop me. You ain't gonna stop me from scratching away them—'

Something about the size of a small horse hit him from the side. One moment he was there above me, the next he was on the ground less than a metre away, kicking and scratching at the ferocious, slavering beast that had pounced on him.

The animal was in a frenzy, using every part of itself to attack the fallen Crowmaster. It was moving too fast for me to make it out clearly, but I could see its gums were pulled back, revealing sharp, yellowing teeth. They snapped furiously at the scarecrow, who hissed and spat and swore, struggling to fend the creature off.

A fist – or it could have been a foot – was thrown from the thrashing mass of teeth and limbs. It caught me across the ear – a glancing blow, but the final straw for my bruised and battered body. My muscles went slack and I began to feel as if I were completely weightless.

Floating on a tide of incoming black, I could hear the Crowmaster squealing and howling as he fought with the animal on his chest. I heard the growling of the beast, the snapping of its wide, vicious jaws. I heard the wheezing of my own breath, flowing unsteadily in and out through my shattered nose. In and out. In and out. In and out.

And through it all – through every terrible sound I heard as I finally lost consciousness – my phone never once stopped ringing.

Chapter Twelve

GUARDIAN ANGELS

I woke up in near darkness, still lying down, but no longer on the ground.

I was on my back on Marion's couch, a blanket covering me from my feet to my chest. The room was draped in shadow, with only the dim light of the flames flickering in the fireplace to ease the gloom. In the half-darkness it took me a few seconds to realise I wasn't alone. Over by the shuttered window, someone stood peering through a gap, their back to me.

There was something else in the room too. I'm not sure how, exactly, but I could sense it there – lurking down on the floor right next to where I was lying. If I listened carefully I could hear the faint wheezing of its breath. It sounded like the breathing of something big, and I guessed it was the animal that had come out of nowhere and attacked the Crowmaster. I probably owed it my life, but the memory of those teeth put me off reaching down and giving it a hug.

Something hit the window with a hollow *thud* and the figure by the shutters took a sudden step backwards, muttering quietly. A sliver of light shone through a gap in the wooden slats, and I caught a glimpse of a face I instantly recognised.

'Ameena?'

She whipped round at the sound of my voice, and her face was lost to the flickering shadows again. On the floor beside me, the hulking shape of the animal shifted. I heard it yawn somewhere close by my ear.

'Hey,' Ameena said. Even in the dark, I could hear her smile. 'You're up.'

'I'm *messed* up,' I corrected, my fingertips cautiously exploring my broken nose and swollen eye sockets. My nostrils were choked up with dried blood, and my voice sounded weirdly nasal when I spoke.

Thud. Something else smacked against the windowpane, making Ameena jump. Down on the floor, I heard the animal give a low growl.

'Maybe I don't want to know,' I began quietly, gesturing towards the creature at my side, 'but what in God's name *is* that?'

'A dog, what do you think?'

'A *dog*?' I spluttered, remembering the beast outside. 'Are we talking about the same animal? Size of a bear? Teeth like a shark?'

'See for yourself.' Ameena shuffled through the darkness and flicked the light switch. The sudden glow from the bulb forced my eyes shut. I blinked rapidly until my vision adjusted, then glanced down into the trusting brown eyes of a very large Great Dane.

It was the same animal, there was no doubt about it. The only difference was now it looked like a friendly – if a bit on the gigantic side – family pet. A far cry from the ferocious, slavering hell-hound I'd seen earlier.

The dog's rough, sandpaper tongue slobbered over my hand as I slowly reached for the little silver disk I could see hanging from its collar. The darkness made it difficult to see, and I had to angle the metal towards the window to read what it said.

'Toto,' I muttered. 'So *you're* Toto.' I let the nametag fall from my fingers. 'Huh. I wonder who the other little guy was.'

'What little guy?' asked Ameena.

'Doesn't matter,' I said, pulling back the blanket and swinging my legs off the couch. Toto stood up, moved out of my way, then flopped back to the floor with a low grunt.

'There's a body upstairs,' Ameena said gravely. 'At least... I think it's a body.'

'I know,' I nodded. 'And it is.'

THUD-AACK! We both heard the glass in the window crack. I didn't really need to ask the question, but I asked it anyway.

'What *is* that?'

Ameena took a deep breath. In the light, I could see how pale and tired she looked. 'A bird,' she said. 'It's a bird. Been flinging itself against the window for the last ten minutes.'

I moved to stand, but my legs weren't strong enough to hold me up. I tried to act as if I'd just been getting comfortable on the couch, but I could tell from her face that Ameena wasn't fooled.

'Just the one?'

'Far as I can tell,' Ameena nodded. 'Why? There aren't more of them, are there?'

I hesitated. 'One or two.'

She gripped her mouth and looked up to the ceiling. Her fingers pressed hard against her jaw, leaving even whiter marks on her already ashen face.

'Great,' she whispered. 'Just great. It had to be birds, didn't it?'

'Not much of an ornithologist, I take it?' I said.

She looked over at me and frowned. 'A what?'

'Ornithologist. They study birds, I think.' I stopped, suddenly doubting myself. 'Or they might be a kind of dentist.'

Ameena stared at me blankly.

'Or is that an orthodontist?'

'What are you *talking about*?' she snapped. 'There's a dead body upstairs, a kamikaze crow out there, and you've got a face like a burst balloon. Why are you going on about dentists?'

I thought about this for a moment. 'I have no idea,' I admitted at last. 'Sorry. Think I'm still a bit dazed.'

'Forget it,' she sighed, slumping down on to the couch next to me. She sat forward, her elbows resting on her knees, her head in her hands. Her left leg bounced up and down, vibrating the old floorboards beneath her.

'So. What happened?' I asked her.

'How should I know? I wasn't here, was I?' she bit back. 'I found you lying out the front with Scooby Doo there trying to lick your face off. Been trying to call you for ages, but you didn't answer. What's up with that? What's the point of having a phone if you don't even answer?'

'I meant at home,' I said softly. It felt like Ameena was teetering on a dangerous edge, and it wouldn't take much to send her plummeting over it. 'What happened with Mum?'

Ameena's leg stopped bouncing. The only movement in the room was the twitching of one of Toto's ears.

'He came out of nowhere,' Ameena said. Her voice was sombre and quiet – matter-of-fact, almost – and it made my heart beat faster. 'Your train had gone, we were just about to get back in the car and then... he was there. He was just *there*. Behind her. Smiling.'

'Go on,' I said.

Ameena rubbed her fingertips hard against her forehead as she continued. 'He picked her up like she was nothing. I tried to stop him, but I was on the other side of the car, and he... he was moving too fast.

'There was a noise, like... I don't know. Just a noise. Like a crash. The car alarm started going off. I didn't realise what had happened to begin with.' Ameena glanced at me, then quickly looked away. 'But then I saw the blood on the windscreen.'

I tried to speak, but my mouth felt full of sand. All I could do was listen.

'He'd cracked the glass. With her head. He'd cracked the glass with her head, and I hadn't even seen him move!'

'What then?' I asked, finding my voice. 'What happened then? How is she? Is she OK?'

Ameena's eyes darted from side to side, as if she was watching the scene replaying before her. 'He ran off,' she said quietly. 'Before I could do anything, he just turned and ran off. He just left her there, lying across the bonnet. Not moving.'

She gave a little cough at the back of her throat and rubbed her sleeve across her eyes. 'Someone must've called an ambulance,' she said. 'They turned up pretty quick. Took us to the hospital by the town.'

'And what are they saying? Is she going to be all right? Have they said anything?'

'She's banged up, but she's stable,' Ameena told me. 'They say she'll be OK. I wouldn't have left her otherwise.'

That was reassuring to hear, but I wasn't as relieved as I expected. I couldn't quite believe it was that simple, that Mum was going to be fine. And I wouldn't believe it, not until I saw her for myself.

I'd done it again. Even when I was trying to keep her safe, I'd put Mum in danger. And Marion too. One of them hurt, one of them dead. All my fault. Mine.

Ameena stood up suddenly and turned away. Her arms were tense by her sides, her bony fingers curled tightly into fists. 'I swear, if I ever see that fat freak again, I'll—'

'You won't,' I said. She turned and I caught the confusion in her red-ringed eyes. 'He's dead,' I explained. 'Really, really dead.'

This seemed to take the wind from her sails a little. She hesitated for a moment, then sat back down on the couch. 'Oh,' she nodded. 'Well... good.'

'He didn't do it. The fat guy. It wasn't him.'

She was back on her feet again. 'Yes it was! I saw him,' she snapped. 'Trust me, I know what I saw, and I saw a fat guy smashing your mum off—'

'It wasn't him,' I repeated, more forcefully this time. I didn't want to hear again what had happened to Mum. 'What you saw – the fat guy – he wasn't real. It was... I'm pretty sure it was, like, a costume.'

'No, Kyle, I've seen costumes before, and this was real!' Ameena argued.

'Trust me,' I told her, 'you've never seen a costume like this.'

She glared at me, still unconvinced. I held her gaze, though, and eventually she shook her head, let out a long sigh, then flopped back down on the couch.

'Well, if that's true, who was wearing it?'

It was my turn to stand up. My legs still felt shaky, but this time I didn't fall down. Toto's eyes followed me as I crossed to the window and looked out through a gap in the shutters. A crack ran the length of the windowpane from top to bottom. A series of smaller cracks spread out from the centre of the glass, presumably where the bird had hit.

The world beyond the window was thick with gloom. A layer of ominous black cloud had rolled across the sky, turning the landscape dark. The trees up on the hillside moved stiffly, jostled and shoved by the wind. With each strong gust they seemed to bow towards the distant mobile phone mast, like ten thousand worshippers pledging loyalty to their god.

I couldn't see the bird that had cracked the window. In fact, for maybe the first time since I'd arrived here, I couldn't see any birds at all.

I felt a warmth on my elbow, and realised Ameena was standing beside me. She was so close her arm was touching mine.

'Hey,' she said, joining me in peeking through the gap, 'crazy bird's gone.'

'Yep,' I nodded. I smiled awkwardly at her, then turned away, feeling my cheeks flush red. Her warmth left my arm and I scurried to where Toto was sleeping on the floor. The dog made a cat-like purr as I scratched behind his ears.

'That's good news, right?' Ameena continued. She was still staring out. She probably hadn't even noticed that I'd moved.

'Yep,' I said again. 'Sure is.'

'Must've been scared off,' she reasoned.

'Must've been,' I agreed. Had she leaned on me like that on purpose, or just so she could see outside?

'Probably that scarecrow over there.'

I nodded. 'Probably.'

Half a second later, my racing brain properly processed what she'd said.

'Ameena!' I cried. *'Get away from the window!'*

'What? Why, what's—?'

I heard the glass shatter and the shutters break almost before it happened. The wood splintered into slivers no bigger than matchsticks. A streak of screeching black tore into the room, catching Ameena on the side of the head and sending her spiralling to the floor.

Sparks were already buzzing through my brain as the bird rocketed towards me. It crossed the room in a heartbeat, flying faster than my startled brain could work. The power was there, but I wasn't quick enough to use it. The bird's black beak pulled open and a piercing screech escaped from within it.

For a fraction of a second I saw myself reflected in its eyes, crouching there, hands in front of my face, like a statue of a coward. And then the bird was too close for me to see anything but black.

Something bumped against my legs from below, knocking me backwards. I felt a sharp, sudden movement; saw a brief blur of speed; and the bird was gone.

Down on the floor, the crow struggled briefly in Toto's jaws. Then, with a crack of bone, the bundle of black feathers went silent and limp. It made a soft *plop* sound as it landed in a messy heap on the floor.

Toto looked lazily up at me, licked his chops, then settled back down to sleep.

I wasted a few seconds getting my breath back. My eyes were still fixed on the dog, who had already begun to snore. My mouth was dry as I swallowed. 'Good boy.'

Ameena and I both stood up at the same time. Blood oozed from a deep gash on her forehead, but she didn't even acknowledge it. She was at the window again, her body tucked out of sight, her head angled so one eye could look out.

I darted over to join her, positioning myself on the other

side of the shattered shutters, so we were standing on opposite sides of the window. I stole a glance outside, and felt an icy band of fear tighten around my throat.

The Crowmaster was prowling around outside the house. He looked a little different from when I'd last seen him. His dungarees had four or five large tears in them, and one of his sleeves had been ripped right off. Whatever damage Toto had done to his body looked to have knitted together again, but he seemed to be limping a little on his impossibly skinny legs.

I glanced back at Toto. 'Good boy,' I whispered again.

The torn clothes weren't the only things to have changed about the Crowmaster. A tall, crooked hat was now pulled down on to his sack-cloth head. It had a wide brim and came to a point at the top. It looked like a hat from a fancy- dress witch's costume, but tatty and torn, and chalky with dust.

On his left shoulder sat a crow. Its claws were dug in deep, and its head was constantly on the move, swivelling this way and that, its eyes scanning the entire area every few seconds.

All of a sudden, the bird's head stopped moving. Its gaze locked on to something on the ground. The Crowmaster skulked towards the object, his own empty eye sockets looking blankly into nowhere.

'What's he doing?' Ameena whispered, as the spindly figure folded at the waist and scooped the item up. He held it up to the bird. Its head cocked side to side as it studied the rectangle of shiny plastic.

I realised what it was before the Crowmaster did, and remembered what had happened just as the birds had been about to finish me off. A shudder of excitement shook my body.

'The number you were calling me on,' I said quietly. 'The mobile.'

'What about it?'

I nodded towards Marion's telephone. It was the old-fashioned kind, with a dial instead of buttons. 'Call it again.'

'What? But—'

'Hurry up,' I hissed. 'I'll explain in a minute.'

I heard Ameena move, but kept my eyes on the scarecrow. After a few moments, the dial of Marion's phone began to click and whirr as Ameena called the number.

If I hadn't been expecting it, I wouldn't have noticed it at first. The crow gave a sudden flap of one wing and its master stumbled ever so slightly, losing his balance for the briefest of moments.

The bird turned its head and lashed out with a sudden peck, taking a chunk right out of the scarecrow's battered hat. The hand holding the plastic object came up, trying to knock the bird away, but this only seemed to make it worse. It gave a menacing *caw* and began to claw furiously at the Crowmaster's shoulder.

'It's ringing,' Ameena told me.

The object in the scarecrow's hand suddenly lit up. I knew the phone would be ringing, but I couldn't hear it over the panicked squawking of the crow. It hurled itself away from the Crowmaster and flapped erratically around the garden, weaving wildly, as if suddenly blinded.

'It's the phone,' I realised. 'However he's controlling them, the phone interferes with it. It breaks his hold over the birds.'

I turned from the window. 'Without the birds, we can beat him!' I cried. 'Don't ask me how, but the phone signal messes him up. We can stop him. We have a weapon!'

The chiming of the ringtone was suddenly behind me. It came from nowhere, grew quickly louder, and then faded just as fast. It stopped completely when the phone disintegrated against the living-room wall, showering the room with pieces of plastic and metal.

Outside, the crow banked down and took up its perch on the Crowmaster's shoulder. The scarecrow's face scraped back into a humourless smile.

'Correction,' said Ameena. 'We *did* have a weapon.'

Chapter Thirteen

CAUGHT BY THE CROWS

Toto's low growl made me turn towards him. He was standing up, his whole body tensed. The short hair on his back stood on end, all the way from his neck to his tail. His ears were raised and his gums were drawn back into a snarl. His dark brown eyes saw nothing but the figure beyond the broken window.

When a bird came hurtling through the hole and into the room, he snapped it from the air, just as he'd done with the last one. It was dead before it hit the ground.

But this one hadn't come alone.

Seven, eight, maybe nine of them – it was hard to tell for sure – came in together in tight formation. They split up inside the room, forcing Toto to circle on the spot, as he tried to keep an eye on them all.

The dog's growl turned into a bark and he lunged at the closest of the birds. His powerful jaws clamped closed on its tail. The crow squawked angrily but pulled itself free, leaving Toto with a mouth full of black feathers.

Over the dog's barking and the screeching of the birds, I heard another sound. It started like a soft ripple of applause, then swelled quickly into an ovation. It came from everywhere — all directions at once — louder and louder, faster and faster with each passing moment.

Ameena had heard the sound too. It was impossible not to. 'What *is* that?' she asked.

'It's more of them. It's more crows,' I replied, shoving her towards the door that led out into the hall. 'Move, move, move!'

The roaring of wings flooded into the room behind us as we stumbled through the open door. Toto barked, yelped and howled, snapping at anything that came close.

'What about the dog?' Ameena asked. 'We can't just leave it there.'

I risked a glance back into the living room. Toto's jaws

were the only part of him I could see. The rest was buried beneath a writhing blanket of black, the carpet below him already awash with blood.

The living-room door gave a firm *click* when I pulled it closed, cutting us off from the scene I knew was about to play out.

'It's too late,' I said. 'There're too many of them!'

As if proving my point, the window in the kitchen shattered, and more of the birds pushed in through the gap. There wasn't even time to pull the kitchen door shut. Instead, I bounded on up the stairs, with Ameena at my back.

'Move!' she screamed. 'Go, go, go!'

I thought back to all the times Ameena had pretended something was chasing us, in order to make me move faster. Mr Mumbles in the garden. A giant snake in the school. I knew that this time was different, though. This time death really was snapping at our heels. Birds were pouring out of the kitchen, moving as one, like a dark and dangerous river flowing towards us.

We thundered up the final few steps and sprinted along the upstairs hallway. In the rooms on either side, the wooden shutters were shaking in their frames, as more and more of the crows fought to force their way through.

I made for the one room I hoped would be safe. There were no shutters on my bedroom window, just the heavy, solid wardrobe wedged in front of the glass. The birds were big, but they wouldn't be able to break through that.

Would they?

Charging at the door, I grabbed for the handle. Ameena staggered into the bedroom behind me, her arms over her head, screaming at me to 'Close it, close it, *close it*!'

With a *slam* that shook the room, I shut out the birds. They threw themselves against the door, hammering into it with a series of short, rapid thuds. The birds were strong, but the door was stronger. It held in place. For the moment.

I turned to Ameena. She was standing by the bed, her hands still held protectively above her head. Her eyes were on the door. They twitched nervously whenever another bird struck against the other side.

'Are you... are you OK?' I asked her. She didn't reply. 'Ameena. Are you—?'

'Of course I'm OK,' she snapped. She brought her arms down and turned away from the door, but it didn't take a psychologist to see through the act.

'It's just, you seem a bit... jumpy.'

'*Jumpy?*' she said with a snort. 'I barely survived an attack by the world's fattest man. I walked and hitchhiked, like, a hundred miles through the night to get here, to find you unconscious on the ground, a dead body in the bedroom, and an eyeless scarecrow dude in the garden.

'Outside that door there're a million birds waiting to eat us, even though, as far as I was aware, birds – actual, proper *bird* birds – don't eat people!' Her voice had been getting higher and higher through her rant. She stopped, took a deep breath, and when she spoke again her tone was much closer to normal. 'So taking all that into account, I think a certain amount of jumpiness is understandable, don't you?'

I nodded, too scared to speak in case she bit my face

off. Ameena was right, she did have every reason to be edgy and nervous, but the fact was I'd never really seen her behave like that before. Even though we'd both faced death a dozen times or more over the past few weeks, none of it had seemed to scare her. Not properly, anyway. She had laughed it all off, and I'd taken confidence from that. Seeing her so frightened frightened me even more.

'Look, I'm fine, OK?' she said with a soft sigh. 'I just... I've never liked birds, that's all.'

'Me neither,' I said. 'One got caught in my hair when I was a kid. It was horrible.'

'Unfortunate,' she said. A grim expression hardened her face. 'One killed my mum.'

'What?' I spluttered. 'God. Really?'

She tried to fight it, but she couldn't. A devilish grin lit up her face. 'Nah, don't be stupid.'

'You're sick!' I said, but inside I was grinning too. Ameena was laughing and joking again, and just like that I could feel my fear ebbing away. Maybe we'd get out of this yet.

The thuds against the door soon became less frequent. They'd stop for twenty or thirty seconds at a time, then catch us by surprise when they started up again. The birds couldn't get inside, but the birds weren't the only thing we had to worry about. I took the high-backed wooden chair from the corner of the room and wedged it against the door handle. If the Crowmaster tried to get in, he wouldn't find it easy.

Ameena slumped down on to the bed and lay back, her eyes closed. For a long few moments I was unsure what to do. Had she really hitched and walked all this way to find me? If she had, she must've been exhausted by now. Letting her have a few minutes' sleep probably wasn't a bad idea.

'So, you going to fill me in on what's been happening?' she asked, not opening her eyes. 'Or do I have to guess?'

'No, I'll tell you,' I said. 'Just not sure where to start.'

'Start by sitting down,' she said, patting the edge of the bed beside her knees. 'You're making the place look untidy.'

I hesitated, then lowered myself down on to the bed as

casually as I could. I didn't want to lean back in case I accidentally brushed against her legs, so I perched right on the edge, using my own leg muscles to keep me hovering a millimetre or two above the blankets. My thighs began to burn almost immediately. I'd have been more comfortable standing.

'Right then,' she said, her eyes still closed. 'I'm all ears.'

I started talking, beginning with the train and ending there in the room with her. I told her about the mega-baby and about Joseph. I told her about the bird at the station, and the one that had shattered the windscreen of Marion's car. I told her all about the dog in the forest, the eyeball under the bed, and the monster in the Marion suit. I stopped short of telling her what the Crowmaster had said – about me being the one who would open the doorway and bring on the end of the world. I would make sure that never happened, so it wasn't something she needed to know.

'So, that's it,' I said, when I'd reached the end. 'That's you up to date.'

Silence.

'You're sleeping, aren't you?' I said.

'No, just thinking.'

'Oh. Thinking what?'

'Thinking we're screwed.'

'Oh. Right. You think?'

'Yep. Unless you've got any bright ideas?'

'They've stopped.'

Ameena opened one eye and squinted at me. 'What?'

'The birds,' I said, tilting an ear towards the door and listening. 'They've stopped. They're not trying to get in.'

We both listened for what felt like ten minutes, but in reality it must have been closer to two. Not a creak, not a sound came from anywhere in the house.

'They've stopped,' Ameena said. She moved her legs and I leapt up off the bed, making room for her to swing her feet down on to the floor. Together we crept closer to the door, both holding our breath as we listened again.

This time we listened for longer. Three minutes. Four minutes. Five. My heart was beating so hard I thought for sure Ameena would hear it, but if she did she didn't let on.

'Think they're gone?' I whispered.

Ameena gave a slight shrug, then slowly reached towards the door. With the knuckle of her middle finger, she gave three short raps on the wood.

Nothing responded. Nothing moved.

'Think they're gone?' I asked again, hardly daring to believe it.

Moving with great care, Ameena eased the wooden chair away from where it was pressed against the door handle. 'Only one way to find out,' she whispered. I saw her hands shake as she wrapped them around the handle. She glanced upwards, steadying her nerve, then inched the door open a crack, just wide enough to see out.

CAAAWRAAAK!

'Nope,' she said, closing the door just in time to stop a fat crow forcing its way in. 'Still there.'

'Damn.'

'That's exactly what I was about to— Good grief, check out your face!' Ameena gasped, as if seeing my injuries properly for the first time. I realised I hadn't had a chance to look at myself since the Crowmaster had smashed my nose, and I could only imagine what I must look like. I could see my own cheeks while still looking straight ahead, which I was fairly sure wasn't normal.

Ameena reached up and gingerly touched the swelling around my eyes. I gave a gasp and pulled back, my nose throbbing with pain at the pressure of her fingers.

'That's got to hurt,' she whistled, her eyes darting over my bruises.

'Does a bit.'

'You look like a big potato man.'

'Thanks.'

A bird battered itself against the other side of the door. Ameena caught my arm and we both took a few steps away. 'Can you do something about it?'

'The birds?'

'Your face.'

'Oh. I... I'm not...' I gave a shrug. 'Dunno. Don't think so.'

'Why not? You healed up from that stabbing in, like, an hour. This isn't as bad as that.'

Ameena was right. After Billy Gibb had stuck a knife into my stomach, my abilities had set to work fixing the wound. I was more or less powerless while I healed, but since the alternative was bleeding to death, I couldn't really complain.

But this was different.

'It just kind of... happened then,' I explained. 'By itself. Nothing's happening this time.'

'Maybe it's a—' A bird thumped against the door. 'Wow, they're annoying. Maybe it's a subconscious thing. You would've died if you hadn't healed up last time. Maybe your subconscious took over and made sure you stayed alive.'

I nodded. 'Could be.'

'But maybe you can do it consciously too. If you focus, or concentrate, or close your eyes and make a wish, or whatever it is you do.'

'Can't hurt, I suppose.'

Ameena's eyes flicked over my swollen face. 'Well... it might a bit.'

I smiled weakly and shut my eyes – although they were so puffed out they were almost closed already. I could feel Ameena watching me, and although I knew my abilities were real, I couldn't help but feel a bit stupid. I had no idea if this was going to work, and for some reason I desperately wanted to impress the girl standing across from me.

Heal, I thought, as clearly and firmly as I could. *Heal up now.*

The pain didn't flinch. It stayed there, like a tight band around my head, squeezing everything together.

'You started yet?' Ameena asked.

'Not yet,' I lied. 'Just about to.'

'Roger that,' she said.

I tried another approach. Maybe if I imagined the bones clicking back into place then they would. Keeping my eyes tight shut, I tried to picture my broken nose straightening itself out; the bones knitting back together into—

The pain exploded like a bomb in the middle of my face. I opened my eyes to find myself on my knees, my cupped hands catching the blood that was flowing from my nostrils.

'You hit me!' I cried. 'Did you... did you *hit me*?'

'Of course I didn't hit you,' Ameena retorted. 'Don't be stupid. Your nose just sort of... moved. By itself.' She gave a faint shudder. 'Wasn't very nice to look at.'

'Wasn't a barrel of laughs from my end, either,' I scowled, wiping a smear of blood from across my lips. I stood up, shaking off the woozy sensation that danced inside my head.

The pain was worse than ever. It burned like fingers of lava, reaching up through my nose and deep into my brain. Ameena chewed her lip as she watched me cross to the bed and sit down.

'Well,' she said, 'it was worth a try, right?'

I glared at her, but didn't reply.

'Any ideas for getting out of here?' she asked.

'Yes.'

'No, me neither. I suppose we could...' She stopped

and looked at me, her head tilted slightly to one side. 'Wait, what did you say?'

'I have an idea for getting out of here,' I told her.

'Excellent!'

'Well, you say that now,' I told her. 'But I don't think you're going to like it.'

Chapter Fourteen

A FALL TO RUINS

'So what, you're just going to *leave* me here?' Ameena demanded. Her voice was higher and more shrill than I'd ever heard it. I'd warned her she wasn't going to like my plan and I'd been right.

'Just for a second,' I assured her. 'The place I'm going is dangerous. I need to check the coast's clear before I take you with me.'

'More dangerous than *here*?' she scoffed, just as another crow crunched against the door.

'Yes,' I said. 'Much more.'

I was still sitting on the bed, looking up at her. Her mouth opened to speak, but either she couldn't think of anything to say, or she couldn't bring herself to say it. Either way, she closed her mouth again and looked away.

'I just...' I stopped, glanced up to the ceiling, then continued. 'It's my fault Mum got hurt. It's my fault that Marion... It's my fault what happened to Marion.' She turned back to look at me, and it took all my willpower not to just look away and start blushing. 'I don't want something happening to you too.'

'So you leave me with a bunch of killer crows?'

'It'll just be for a second,' I promised. 'And then I'll come back.'

She chewed on her lip again and looked over to the door. When she looked back, her face was several shades paler.

'You'd better.'

I stood up. 'I will.'

Ameena hesitated, then gave a short, reluctant nod of her head. 'So,' she said, 'how does this work?'

'The place I'm going, it's called the Darkest Corners,' I explained. 'It's where they go when they're forgotten. All the imaginary friends. It's where they all go.'

'That's where you went with the girl and the doll?'

'Yeah,' I said. 'But that wasn't the first time I've been there. I can just sort of take myself there. It's hard to explain, but that world's a lot like this one. A building here is the same building there.'

'What, exactly the same?'

'Well, yeah. No. Sort of,' I said. 'But a bit more run down. And with a load more monsters.'

'Sounds lovely,' said Ameena grimly.

'It isn't. But maybe there's a way out over there. We're trapped in this room, but the birds are here in this world, not that one. If we can go there and escape from the house, I can bring us back a mile away from here and the crows won't even know we've left the room.'

'OK,' Ameena said, even though she was shaking her head. 'Go for it. But hurry.'

'I'll be quick,' I said. 'Don't go anywhere.'

A half-smile pulled at the corner of Ameena's mouth. 'Funny. Now scat.'

* * *

I might not have been able to heal myself, but transporting myself to the Darkest Corners was becoming almost second nature. It took me just a few seconds to make the feeling of electricity zip through my head, and just a few more to focus on one of the flickering blue sparks. There was a brief sensation, like a wind howling through my head, and the world around me changed.

It was dark, but then it was always dark there. What was more surprising was that instead of standing inside a house, I was floating three or four metres above the ruins of one.

I didn't stay floating for long.

Had the building collapsed recently, my landing would have been worse than it actually was. Luckily for me the house seemed to have fallen down years ago. The moss and grass that had grown over its remains broke my fall a little, and saved me from any broken bones.

Still, it hurt. A lot. I lay there, half hidden by the grass and debris, willing my body to get up. But the pain brought with it an exhaustion like none I'd ever known, and for a long time my body ignored my requests and just did its own thing.

Eventually, the thought of Ameena stuck back in the house stirred my muscles into moving. A dull ache across my shoulders became sharp and stabbing as I pushed myself up on my arms. The moss beneath me was slippery and wet. It took me three attempts to get to my feet, and two more tries before I managed to stay there.

The glow from a fat, full moon slipped through a gap in the clouds and cast a silvery glow over my surroundings. The faint light picked out details that swept away any doubts I may have had that this was the same house as the one I'd just left.

Most of the walls had long since fallen down, but a few hadn't crumbled all the way. I could make out the shape of Marion's kitchen. The enormous cooker she'd made dinner on stood cold and silent in the corner. Weeds grew around its iron feet and crawled up over the oven door, binding it shut.

I clambered past the oven, and out through the gap in

the wall where the back door should have stood. Once outside the building's boundary, I began scrabbling in the rocks at my feet, pushing them aside and ripping up the grass and weeds below.

I don't know why I was so determined to find it. Maybe I still had doubts. Maybe I couldn't believe that even here, in this hellish place, Marion's house could be quite so decayed. Or maybe I just didn't want to believe it, because if it was true – if this really was Marion's house – then that meant...

I tore out a clump of weeds, and there it was. It was caked with soil, and scarred by years of neglect, but even in the half-light of the moon the colour was unmistakeable.

Yellow.

Follow the yellow brick road.

Tears suddenly filled my eyes, swimming the world out of focus. I thought of Ameena, stuck in that room, death waiting just beyond the door to claim her. I was supposed to make the jump back to her. I was supposed to go back and save her. I'd promised. But if I went back there now, I wouldn't be inside the room, I'd be outside the house. There'd be no way for me to get back to her.

I realised I was still holding fistfuls of weeds. I let them fall, and slowly stood up. My eyes went up to the spot where I had first appeared. Just up there, and a whole world away, Ameena would be pacing the floor.

Even now, I'd been gone longer than I'd told her I would. Would she be worrying yet? Would she be thinking I'd been killed? Or worse, that I'd just abandoned her?

I wiped my tears on the back of my clenched fists. I had to go back. Even if it meant appearing right in the middle of the crows and fighting my way up to the bedroom, I would do it. There was no way I was just going to leave her on her own.

I closed my eyes and made the sparks flash through me, but before I could trap one, a hand caught me by the shoulder and spun me roughly round.

Flicking my eyes open, I instinctively raised my fists, ready for whatever monster I was about to encounter. But what I found myself facing wasn't a monster. Not on the outside, anyway. It was a man.

It was my dad.

'Well now,' he smiled, his hand still on my shoulder, 'fancy seeing you all the way out here.'

Pulling back, I batted his grip away. A flash of mock surprise passed across his face, only to be replaced by his usual self-satisfied smirk.

I hated him. Hated the way he towered above me and made me feel small. Hated his broad shoulders and muscular arms that looked as if they could snap me like a twig. Hated his short, dark hair and his craggy, unshaven face.

And most of all I hated the fact that when he looked at me, I could see my own features in his. The resemblance between us – even I had to admit – was uncanny. And that made me feel sick.

I didn't want to be related to this man. I didn't want to have anything to do with him ever again. All the bad things that had happened in the past few weeks – all the pain and the fear and the *death* – were down to him. And now he was smiling at me. Grinning. And that made me hate him all the more.

'What do you want?' I demanded through gritted teeth.

'Hey, what's the matter?' he said, sticking his bottom lip out, like a baby about to burst into tears. 'No "How are you? How you been?" or anything?' He held his arms wide and stepped in closer. 'Come on. Give your old man a hug.'

'Touch me and I'll kill you,' I warned. I was shocked to hear the words come out of my mouth, but in that instant I knew I meant them. After everything he'd done to me – to Mum – I knew there was a part of me that would love to see him burn.

He hesitated, and this time the flicker of surprise on his face appeared genuine. He recovered quickly, and the smirk was back on his face in moments. But he didn't touch me.

'Well, what kind of way is that to talk to your—'

'I should kill you anyway,' I snarled. 'The Crowmaster. You sent him after me, didn't you? You sent him.'

'Guilty as charged,' he said, beaming proudly. 'Although I told him to smash your mum's skull in first.' He placed the back of his hand next to his mouth, as if sharing some great secret. 'Between you and me, she's had it coming for a while.'

I hurled myself at him, driving a shoulder hard into his stomach. I was screaming – no, *roaring* – as I kicked my feet against the stone and shoved forward.

He gave a low groan, and for one triumphant moment I thought I'd hurt him. But the groan became a chuckle, and the chuckle became a laugh. He was standing his ground with ease, my charge not making him take so much as a single step backwards.

'Easy there, kiddo!' he snorted. 'Almost creased my shirt.'

I swung wide with a fist and drove it into his side, right below his ribcage. It made a satisfying *thump*, but his only reaction was to laugh louder.

'Now you're just being silly,' he said, and the lightness in his voice sent tremors of rage right through me.

'You think I can't hurt you?' I barked, leaping back from him. The electrical surge of my powers burned like white fire behind my eyes.

'What, you think you can?' He winked with his left eye, and at the same time his right arm began to move. His open hand caught me across the side of the face. The slap made a sound like the cracking of a whip, and an alarm started wailing in my left ear.

The strike shocked me and made me lose my focus. My dad's eyes were alive with a shimmering darkness. His hand was already drawing back, opening up, getting ready to rain down another blow.

'Go on then,' he said, punctuating the sentence with another *smack* that made my teeth rattle and my cheek burn. 'Do it. Hurt me, tough guy.'

I stumbled back, my arms shielding my head from another attack. He was laughing again – a deep, booming laugh he seemed to spit all the way from the bottom of his stomach.

The buzzing inside my head exploded outwards, as I

raced to visualise his legs snapping in two. 'OK,' I growled, picturing the cracking and the tearing as his bones broke and ripped outwards through his thigh muscles. 'You asked for it.'

The image solidified in my mind, clearer than anything I could ever remember imagining before. Everything, right down to the shock and fear on his face was frozen there behind my eyelids. Lucid. Crystal clear.

But not actually happening.

I kept the image in my head. Focused on it. Filled the sparks with every detail of that picture, sent them rushing towards him. But still he didn't budge. The power was roaring through me. The mental picture was there.

So why wasn't it working? Why wouldn't he fall?

He moved with the speed and grace of a big cat, leaping a mound of broken bricks and landing directly in front of me. I tried to pull back, but his hand was suddenly in my hair, bunched into a fist, holding my head in place.

'Oh, didn't I mention?' he said, smiling innocently. 'You don't work over here.' He leaned in close enough for me to smell the stale sourness of his sweat. 'Here in this world, you're nothing. You're nothing special at all.'

With a low grunt, he threw me backwards, releasing his grip and letting me drop like a dead weight on to the muddy grass. A dull ache jabbed at my hip as I landed on top of the lighter Marion had left me with. Under normal circumstances the pain would have bothered me, but right now it was the last thing on my mind.

There was a faint *chink* as my dad unclipped the thick metal buckle of his belt, and then he was back standing over me, very slowly and very deliberately wrapping the thick belt strap around one of his fists. With each loop over his knuckles, the leather gave a foreboding *creak*.

'Now,' he said, pressing the wrapped fist into the palm of his other hand, 'let Daddy show you how it *should* be done.'

Chapter Fifteen

INTO THE BIRDHOUSE

'**W**ait!' I yelped, shuffling backwards. 'You need me. The Crowmaster told me everything. You need me alive.'

'Alive, yes. Uninjured? Not necessarily,' my dad said. He walked slowly forward, keeping pace with me. 'Took me almost a whole day to travel all the way up here, but I knew you'd make the jump over eventually. I wanted to be here. Waiting.'

'You came all this way just to beat me up?'

'Partly that,' he nodded. 'Partly that. Mostly, though, I wanted to offer you one more chance to pick the right side.' He looked off into the middle distance, then back to me. 'I know I said I wouldn't offer again, but I felt bad about that,

Kyle, I really did. You're my son, I shouldn't have given up on you so quickly.'

My back hit the partially collapsed wall that would have made up one side of Marion's kitchen. I had no choice but to stop. My dad stepped closer so his feet were next to mine. The full moon sat directly behind him, casting a ghostly white halo around his head.

'So *this* is my final offer,' he continued, creaking the leather around his fist to hammer home his point. 'There's a war coming, Kyle. Help me. Work with me. And I promise we'll rule the world.'

I didn't reply. There was something in the tone of his voice I hadn't heard before. Was it... desperation?

'So,' he asked, with something bordering on compassion in his smile, 'what do you say?'

'You're scared, aren't you?' I said. Though his features didn't move, the warmth drained right out of his face. 'Whatever your plan is – whatever you're going to do – you can't do it without me, can you? You're scared it's all falling apart.'

'Scared?' He rolled the word around in his mouth as he said it, as if tasting every letter. 'What could I possibly be scared of?'

I pushed myself up using the wall for support. He didn't make any move to try to stop me. 'Me,' I answered. 'You're scared of me.'

Just as I'd hoped, he hurled back his head and laughed. It was all for show, like a lot of the things he did, but I'd been counting on him doing it. I knew he wasn't afraid of me.

But he should have been.

I swung hard with a rock I'd taken from the ground. He must've seen my arm move from the corner of his eye, because his laughter caught in his throat. Too late. The chunk of stone vibrated in my hand as it battered solidly against the side of his head.

A noise that was halfway between a gasp and a growl escaped his lips. He staggered sideways, his hand flying to his eye socket where the rock had caught him. His undamaged eye turned on me, hatred burning in its dark centre.

'I'll never help you,' I told him. My insides felt like half-set jelly, so I was amazed by how confident my voice sounded. 'I might not have any abilities here, but in my world I do, and I'll use them to stop anything you send after me, including the Crowmaster. Understood?'

'You've just made the biggest mistake of your life,' my dad hissed. Trickles of blood were seeping through his fingers. I couldn't bring myself to feel bad about it. 'I know you better than you know yourself, son. I've been planning this since the day you were born. You'll help me. You'll make that whole world burn. Whether you mean to or not.'

'Don't count on it,' I told him, and before he could answer, I caught hold of a spark that flitted past behind my eyelids, and left that hellish place behind.

It was brighter back in the real world, but not much. The layer of cloud that covered the sky had grown thicker in my absence, blocking out even more of the sun's light. A raw January wind whistled around me, nipping at my ears and nose.

But at least the wind was the only thing nipping at me. Even though I'd arrived back outside Marion's house, I couldn't see a single bird in the sky. That was either very good news, or very bad. Good because it meant I wasn't currently having my tongue torn out, but bad because if the birds weren't out here, then they were probably all waiting inside.

Ducking down low, I scurried over to the kitchen window and took a peek through the shattered pane. The kitchen had been virtually destroyed. The hanging pots lay scattered on the floor. The table where Marion and I had eaten our dinner was covered by a layer of shattered glass. All the little knick-knacks and ornaments that had sat on all the little shelves had been knocked over, smashed, or both.

And over everything – on every surface – were feathers. Dozens and dozens of greasy black feathers.

But no birds.

I couldn't remember if the back door creaked, so I decided not to take the chance. The last thing I wanted to do was announce my presence and bring the birds flocking from wherever in the house they currently were. Instead, I carefully picked the larger slivers of glass from the wooden frame, and sat them down on the ground.

The wind grew around me as I worked. It only took twenty or thirty seconds to clear the worst of the glass, but by the time I had finished my fingers were numb with cold. I cupped them to my mouth and breathed on them for a few seconds, readying myself for what came next.

My entrance wasn't as stealthy as I'd hoped. I pushed myself up on the narrow window ledge and kicked against the roughcast stone wall with both feet. As I leaned my body forward into the kitchen, my legs were forced to bicycle-kick in thin air for a moment. I hung there, feet flailing frantically, as I realised I was sliding headfirst into the house.

There was no way to stop. My arms buckled and my legs swung up and I was helpless to prevent myself face-planting on to the glass-covered table. I slid right over the top, bringing the table with me as I crunched on to the hard kitchen floor.

It probably hurt, but I had no time to dwell on it. I was on my feet in a heartbeat, readying myself for the crows. They were sure to have heard my entrance. They'd be here any second.

As I stood there, eyes locked on the door, my ankle nudged against something. I lashed out instantly with the foot, not taking any chances. The metal soup pot spun across the floor until it hit the stove with a hollow *clang*.

Cursing myself for being so jumpy, I reached down and grabbed another cooking pot. It was a hefty bit of cookware, and I needed both hands to swing it properly, but I was ready to bet it'd be an effective weapon against an oncoming bird.

Probably wouldn't be so handy against a hundred of them, of course, but I tried not to think about that too much. It was better than nothing. Just.

The expected rush of flapping wings didn't happen, and I crept over to where the kitchen led out into the hall. Tucking myself in close to the doorframe, I risked a peek round the corner.

The hall looked much like the kitchen. The floor was covered in broken trinkets and torn phone books and the shattered remnants of what had been Marion's life. The same feathers were here, scattered haphazardly over the carpet and up the dark, narrow stairs.

My legs were trembling as I tiptoed across the hall to the bottom of the steps. Halfway there, I heard the sounds I had been dreading: a soft *caw* and the rustle of oily wings.

The sounds hadn't come from the hallway, and they hadn't come from up the stairs. But where had they come from? I stood in the middle of the floor, completely in the open, but frozen to the spot, listening for the noises to come again.

I didn't have to wait long. An inquisitive croak to my right made me spin to face the living-room door. A fat, black crow sat just inside the room, its back to me. It had a lump of dark red meat pinned beneath its claws. The meat made a sticky *schlop* sound as the bird's beak tore strip after strip away. After every bite, the crow tipped back its head and let the meat fall down into its gut.

I gripped the handle of the cooking pot until my knuckles turned white. I wanted to bring the pot down on the bird's head – to squish the thing into the carpet. To make it pay for what it had done to the dog. And had I not been so terrified, I might have done just that.

Instead, I snuck over to the door, picking my steps carefully, trying not to make any sound. I made it without alerting the bird, but now I was less than a metre away from the thing. It had its head down, ripping into the meat. If it craned its neck back now to swallow another bite, it would surely see me.

With no time to lose, I reached for the handle. As the door began to pull closed, the bottom of it brushed against the carpet.

The sound startled the bird. It released its grip on the meat and flapped into the air. Twisting round, it fixed me with its glassy gaze and opened its beak wide. Small lumps of half-chewed flesh still stuck in its throat, and I knew that if I didn't act fast, the next thing to go down that gullet would be me.

Panicking, I pulled the door closed much harder than I'd meant to. The slam seemed to vibrate the walls and floor, and echo around the house. There was no way the other birds wouldn't hear it, but that no longer mattered. If, as I suspected, the Crowmaster saw through the eyes of his minions, then it was too late for stealth. The bird had seen me, so the Crowmaster would know exactly where I was.

The fact the birds didn't come whooshing down the stairs didn't do anything to comfort me. If anything, it made my heart beat even faster. I should've been glad, but the fine hairs on the back of my neck stood on end as I realised nothing was coming for me.

The birds were all up there, and they now knew I'd escaped, so why weren't they coming? Why weren't...?

I let the pot fall; took the steps three at a time. The smell from Marion's remains hung in the air, thick and putrid and rotten enough for me to smell even through my blocked and broken nose as I powered up the final few stairs and on to the upper landing.

Empty. The upstairs hallway was empty!

I ran to the far end, shouting Ameena's name, but knowing she wouldn't answer. I knew the door would be open. Knew the room would be empty. Knew I'd been gone too long.

A tightness gripped my stomach and spread out through my body until my muscles were standing in knots. An emotion I couldn't even name – not rage, not terror, but something much more – boiled my blood in my veins. The scream of something primal shook the walls, and although the sound was completely alien to me, I knew I was the one making it.

He had taken her. The Crowmaster. I'd promised her she would be safe, and *he had taken her*. I knew that handing control of my powers over to anger wasn't a good idea, but not a single part of me cared. I had left her alone, and she had been taken. Another bad thing that was all my fault. Another person I cared about hurt because of me.

No more. Never again.

I turned on my heels and made for the door, the sparks glowing so brightly inside me I swear they lit up the room.

Just before I left the bedroom behind, I heard it. A knocking from inside the wardrobe. Soft and cautious.

My stomach tightened, ejecting a breath that was halfway between a laugh and a cry. I scolded myself for doubting her. Ameena was more than able to handle herself. What had I been worried about?

'It's OK,' I said, about-turning back into the room, 'the coast's clear. The birds have gone.'

And then, without even pausing to consider the consequences, I took hold of the handles and pulled both wardrobe doors wide open.

Chapter Sixteen

FLAMING CLOSE

In hindsight, it's easy to say I should have been more careful. I shouldn't have just bashed on the way I did. I should have waited for Ameena to answer. I should have thought it through.

I *should've* done a lot of things. What I shouldn't have done is open those doors.

They'd broken the window and punched right through the thin plywood at the back of the wardrobe. I pulled the wardrobe open expecting to find Ameena. What I found were birds. Six, eight, maybe twelve of them – it was impossible to tell. They were stacked on top of one another, the blackness of their bodies merging them into one big, feathery shape.

As the doors opened, the crows exploded into life. I

stepped back, ducked, but they were already on me, flapping and shrieking like miniature demons. Claws tore at me through my clothing. A beak snapped shut just centimetres from my eyes. I twisted and writhed, batting at the birds with my fists, but they moved too fast for me to land a solid punch.

'Getoff-getoff-getoff!' I cried, throwing myself around like a rag doll. Every direction I turned, there was another bird, scratching me, pecking me, beating its wings in my face. I thought of Marion, and of the unnamed dog up there on the hill. Their bones had been virtually pecked clean, their flesh consumed by birds just like those on me now. Was that how it was going to end? Was I destined to wind up a mound of bloody scraps, miles from home in an unfamiliar house?

I crashed out of the room and into the hallway, clawing back at the crows, trying to catch them, pull them off me. One of the birds made a lunge for my hand. I heard its beak snap shut and felt a searing pain in the web of skin between my thumb and index finger.

'That hurt!' I snarled. I wriggled like some demented snake. Twisting and thrashing. And as the pain burned in my hand, a panic rose like acid in my stomach. I was going to die. *I was going to die!*

The stairs came upon me suddenly and I lost my footing, toppling sideways and hitting the steps hard. Two of the crows burst open with a sickening *pop* as my full weight came down on them. The others backed off, remaining up at the top of the stairs while I bumped and clattered my way down to the bottom.

Dazed, I somehow managed to roll to my feet. I grabbed for the cooking pot I'd dropped earlier; turned with it; swung wildly. A charging bird went down with a satisfying *clang*, but the others were already making their way down the stairs.

Once again, I let the pot fall. I ducked into the kitchen, through the back door, and out into the world beyond. All the while a drumbeat of greasy wings followed close behind.

I pulled the back door behind me, just before the crows

could make it out. The window was still broken, of course, but hopefully it'd take their bird brains a few seconds to realise that fact.

I could see smoke pouring from the broken living-room window. The crows had trashed the room when they'd charged through it, knocking everything to the floor. A toppled armchair had landed in the fire and was now blazing brightly on the floor. I looked up at the old timber house. It wouldn't stand a chance.

And nor would I, if I didn't think of something fast. If only I had the mobile phone. It had proved to be the best weapon against the crows – maybe if I still had it I wouldn't be in this mess. If only the Crowmaster hadn't smashed it. If only...

The forest on the hillside seemed to draw my eyes to it. I took a few faltering steps in that direction, as if being pulled in. There was something about the trees. Something that my subconscious had already realised, but which the rest of my brain was struggling to...

To...

My God, I thought. *Of course!*

I hesitated just long enough to get my bearings, then broke into a run. Hope surged through me, powering my exhausted legs onwards up the hill, away from the house. Behind me, the crows were already beginning to find their way out through the broken kitchen window. That was the bad news.

The good news loomed in the distance ahead of me, standing tall and rigid and shiny above the treetops.

I sprinted towards the forest, headed in the direction of the mobile phone mast. I scrambled up the hill on all fours, using grass and bracken for handholds where I could, digging my fingers into the dirt when there was nothing to grab on to. My feet kicked furiously, slipping more often than not on the slick, muddy soil. It was slow progress, and by the time I'd made it in among the trees, my legs were caked with damp dirt.

I wasted half a second looking back over my shoulder. The birds were still flying around the outside of the house, soaring and diving in ever-widening circles. They were searching, I realised. Searching for me.

It took some effort to stop myself cheering. If they were searching, then they didn't know where I was. I'd done it. I had escaped!

For now, at least.

Ducking low, I pushed further into the woods, not walking, but not quite running, either. The smells of the forest closed in around me. The sweet scent of pine. The faint eggy stink of rotting leaves on boggy ground.

The forest had its own soundtrack too. The swishing of branches, the gasping of the wind, the melodic tweeting of distant birds – birds I could only hope had no plans to kill me. The sights, the smells, the sounds, they all combined to give the impression the woods were another world, unrelated to the one beyond its borders.

My trousers were wet from the grass. They slowed me down, but I tried to keep up my semi-running pace as I clambered over the trunk of an uprooted tree and hauled myself further up the hill.

Reaching the top of a low ridge, I turned and looked back the way I'd come. I could make out parts of the house through gaps between some branches. The fire had caught hold and most of the upstairs looked to be alight. I was relieved to see the birds were still flapping around the burning building, still too stupid to figure out where I'd gone.

Wheezing and breathless, I half sat, half perched on the trunk of another fallen tree, and tried to figure out what to do next. I'd only come into the forest in the hope that the mobile phone mast would have the same effect on the crows as my phone had, but now the birds weren't following me, getting to the mast didn't seem to matter. Finding Ameena, that was what was important. But where would the Crowmaster take her?

I don't know how long I sat there, half watching the crows buzzing like flies around the smouldering skeleton of Marion's home, half just enjoying the feeling of air flowing freely into my lungs. All the while I was thinking. Wondering. Where would he take her? *Why* would he take her?

An acrid smokiness had flavoured the air in the forest now. It mingled with the other scents. The pine. The rotting leaves.

Despite the distance, if I listened carefully, I could even

make out the occasional faint hiss and crackling of the flames as they consumed what little was left of the house. Like the smell of the smoke, the sounds felt like alien invaders, out of place among the swishing of branches, the gasping of the wind and the melodic...

My stomach twitched and my throat tightened. The birds I'd heard twittering in the distance were twittering no longer. Their music had given way to an empty, chilling silence.

I stood up slowly, being careful not to make any sudden movements. My head stayed level, facing straight ahead, but my eyes pointed upwards into the shadowy treetops. I didn't want to find it, but the sinking feeling in my gut told me I would. Sure enough, there it was.

It was perched high up on a branch, its black eyes fixed on me. I tried to act as if I hadn't spotted it. Tried to appear as calm as I could, while inside my heart tried to punch a hole right through my chest.

The crow extended its wings and I braced myself, expecting it to make its dive. It quickly folded them in against its back, though, and even as I began to edge away from it, the bird made no move to follow.

I made it several metres further up the hill, still walking backwards, still watching the bird. I could barely make it out now, its dark shape blending with the shadows of the tree. Not that I was complaining, but I couldn't understand why it wasn't coming after me. Why wasn't it giving chase?

The reason hit me like a kick to the stomach, forcing a gasped 'No!' out through my trembling lips. I couldn't see Marion's house any more, but I didn't have to see it to know the birds were no longer circling. I could *hear* them sweeping up the hillside, tearing through the forest, a tornado of thrashing black. The bird hadn't attacked for one simple reason. It was waiting for backup.

Cursing myself, I turned and scuttled up the hill, through the trees, dragging myself along by low branches and exposed roots. I shouldn't have stopped. I should never have rested.

But I *had* stopped. I *had* rested. And as death closed in on a hundred beating wings, I feared it would be the last stupid mistake I ever got the chance to make.

Chapter Seventeen

DEMON IN DISGUISE

The faster I tried to run, the more the trees fought to slow me down. Bare, spindly branches whipped at me, tearing at my hands and face like tiny claws. The steep forest floor seemed to be growing around me, wrapping itself around my wrists and ankles, gripping me, holding me back. I didn't even try to delude myself. There was no way I was outrunning the birds.

A nano-second before I heard the first *caw*, the sparks electrified my skin. The sudden shock made my legs kick out and I leapt like a startled frog, covering over two metres in a single bound. Right behind me, the first of the following crows crashed, beak-first, against the hillside.

Another jolt buzzed through me, and this time I was

hurled to my right. A second bird failed to pull up in time. It gave a startled *squawk* as it slammed into the scrub beside me.

Slowing only to boot the beast as hard as I could, I kept moving. The ground was rising sharply, becoming almost a wall of dirt, held together by the roots of a huge tree that towered above me.

Kicking my feet in against the muck, I caught a trailing root and climbed. One metre. Two. I was over halfway up the curved wall when the next bird came at me. Again, the electrical buzz zapped through me, but this time there was nowhere to go. I could only keep climbing as the crow swooped at me, its curved claws outstretched.

I ducked my head, protecting my face. Pain exploded at the top of my spine as the crow's talons dug into my neck. Clinging on to the root with one hand, I threw the other back over my head, fist clenched. The punch missed the bird and threw my balance off. Helplessly, I spun so I was facing away from the embankment.

For a moment I thought the forest was alive. Birds moved

on almost every tree, hopping over one another, pushing others aside as they jostled for position. An audience, fighting among themselves for the best view.

I spun further, still holding on with one hand. I cried out as the crow dug its claws in deeper, and almost didn't hear the irritated croak the bird gave. I quickly realised why the bird had made the sound. My half-turn had bumped the thing against the wall of soil.

I gritted my teeth and twisted at the waist, swinging myself back around towards the wall until I could press my feet flat against the steep curve. The bird gripped tighter and the wave of pain almost made the muscles in my arm give up. But I clung on, knowing I'd probably only get one chance to rid myself of this nasty pain in the neck.

Roaring, I kicked with my feet and swung out with my free arm, hurling myself around in a half-circle so my back was rushing towards the wall. At the same time, I brought my head sharply up and back.

Realising what was about to happen, the crow released its grip. By then it was too late. It dropped down below my shoulders just as my back was driven against the tightly packed dirt. The bird gave a strangled cry, then dropped past my legs and rolled clumsily down the hill.

I had no idea if it was dead, but nor did I have any intention of stopping to find out. Gripping the tree root with both hands, I clambered up the rest of the embankment, the thrashing of wings already filling the forest behind me.

With my muscles burning, I heaved myself up over the top of the wall. The ground here was flatter, sloping only very slightly upwards. I scrambled forward on my hands and knees, my tired legs not able to give me the explosive start I hoped for. My right hand slipped on something wet and I almost landed face-first in a quivering mound of reddish-brown flesh and greying fur.

It was the dog – well, part of it, at least – that first dog I'd encountered here in the forest only yesterday. The dog I'd seen torn to shreds. The dog I had at the time assumed must be...

Toto. The word winked up at me from the dull grey metal

of the animal's nametag, which poked out from a fold in the blood-soaked fur.

Toto.

Toto. Toto. Toto.

The word repeated in my head, over and over, like the steady clattering of an express train.

Toto. Toto. Toto.

Toto. Toto. Toto.

How could this be Toto? If this *was* Marion's dog, then what about the one at the house? The one that had appeared from nowhere at just the right moment and saved me from—

The crows. In that brief moment of confusion, I had forgotten the crows.

They suddenly filled the space around me; clawing, screeching, snapping, croaking, flapping, biting at me.

Terror gave me the strength to push against them, hands over my head, until I was on my feet. Blindly I staggered onwards, tears streaking my face, a hundred different agonies stabbing through my skin.

Panic smothered my power and kept me from using it. All I could do was keep my head low and try to run, but even that proved too difficult. With the birds covering every part of me, I fell forward on to the forest floor.

I couldn't see through the mass of beaks and wings and feathery bodies, couldn't hear a thing above their crazed screeching. I was lost in a blizzard of black, inching along on my hands and knees, waiting for one final, inevitable strike.

But then, without warning, the crows moved away. They pulled back, leaping off me and curving upwards to be swallowed by the darkening sky. I crawled forward, every centimetre of my skin awash with my blood, until a pair of dirty black boots blocked my path.

I stopped crawling and for a moment just lay there, looking at those boots. This was it then. It was over. He had found me.

I rolled on to my side and managed to turn my head enough to look up. The face that looked back was not the one I had expected to see.

'Come on, get up, we need to move,' Ameena urged, bending down and catching me by the hand. She pulled hard, but her grip slipped on my blood-soaked skin, and my arm dropped back down on top of me.

The world blurred and turned shades of grey, like an out-of-focus old movie. A tingling, like pins and needles, prickled at the back of my head. It wasn't my abilities this time. It was sleep. Or unconsciousness. Or something more.

I could feel Ameena's hand on my face. It brushed against my cheek, leaving behind a tickly imprint of her palm. The numbness in my skull eased, and a vague focus returned to the world just in time for Ameena to slap me again.

My cheek was still burning as she grabbed me by the shoulders and dragged me into a sitting position. I could make out her face close to mine, her eyes wide. Panicked. Bloodshot.

'Wake up, dammit,' she shouted, raising her open hand. 'They'll be coming back. Wake up!'

'O-OK,' I muttered, 'just *please...* stop hitting me.' I leaned a hand on her shoulder. 'Help me up.'

'No time,' she replied, glancing up into the treetops, 'I need you moving on your own steam if we're getting out of here.' She looked me up and down, and I could see the doubt in her eyes. 'Can you heal yourself?'

I frowned. Even this tiny movement sent pain rippling across my face and down through my body. Far overhead, a crow *cawed*.

'Let me rephrase that,' Ameena said, the urgency obvious in her voice. 'Heal yourself. Now.'

'I... I don't think...'

She leaned in closer still, close enough for me to smell the Crowmaster's stink on her clothes. 'Listen, kiddo,' she hissed. 'I'll spell it out. We. Are. Going. To. *Die*. Both of us. Here and now.' She peered up into the trees again, then back down at me. 'And your mum next. He's going to finish what he started. And then, when he's done with her, he's...'

Ameena continued to talk, but I was no longer listening. I was concentrating on my wounds, feeling the pain from every one of them, making a map of every injury. I had healed before, and I was sure I could do it again, if I could only figure out how.

I tried to focus on each individual pain at the same time, imagined the wounds knitting together, sealing shut. An itchiness crept across my skin, up my arms, around my neck, and down my back. Steadily, the itching grew in intensity, until my whole body felt like it was burning.

'I can't!' I hissed, feeling that my skin would blister any second. 'I can't do it.'

'Come on,' Ameena said, and her voice was little more than a growl at the back of her throat. 'I need you healthy.'

The words, and the way she said them, made me hesitate. Her eyes seemed to bore into me, wide and bloodshot. That smell from her clothes flooded my nostrils.

The smell of the Crowmaster.

'What do you mean, *you need me healthy*?' I asked her. 'Need me for what?'

Her pause was so short it was barely noticeable, but it was there. 'So we can, you know, *run for our lives*?'

I pushed backwards on my hands, studying her face. 'The birds flew away,' I said, partly to her and partly to myself. 'When you arrived, they all flew away. Why would they do that?'

'How should I know?' she shrugged. 'Now come on, if you're not going to fix yourself we need to move.'

She held a hand out to me, but I didn't take it. My eyes searched her face. She looked like Ameena. She spoke like Ameena. But Marion had looked and sounded like Marion right up until the point the scarecrow had burst out of her skin.

'Get away from me,' I said, my voice shaking.

Ameena raised her eyebrows. 'Say what?'

'You're him,' I spat. 'Aren't you?'

The thing that looked like Ameena shuffled forward on its knees. 'What are you talking about?' it demanded. 'We don't have time for this.'

I let it get closer. Didn't stop it closing in. Didn't resist when its hand caught me by the arms. The monster opened Ameena's mouth, spoke with Ameena's voice, but I had no interest in hearing anything it said. With a sharp jerk of my leg, I drove my knee hard against its jaw.

The thing cursed and swore like Ameena would, but I was beyond being fooled. I knew the truth – the horrible, sickening, heart-breaking truth.

I couldn't watch it happening, though. I couldn't sit there and watch the Crowmaster tear his way free from inside the skin of my friend. I *wouldn't* watch it.

With a final kick against what had once been Ameena's shoulder, I sent the thing sprawling backwards over the embankment and rolling down the hill.

And then, finding strength from who-knows-where, I got to my feet and ran further into the forest, Ameena's voice crying, 'Kyle, come back!' as I made my way up the hill.

Chapter Eighteen

SNEAK ATTACK

I stumbled clumsily through the woods, clattering into trees, tripping on weeds, barely staying upright. I was no longer even sure where I was running to, but I knew exactly what I was running from.

She'd been my friend. Maybe my *only* friend. And now she was... she was... I couldn't bring myself to think about it.

I staggered on, but at every step I was bombarded by another image of Ameena. Her wide grin that made her nose crinkle up. Her boots under my mum's coffee table. The feeling of her shoulder against mine as we'd looked out through Marion's window.

I heard the monster shout with Ameena's voice

somewhere behind me – not too far away. A knot of anger bunched my stomach up tight, and my feet decided to stop moving all by themselves.

The voice called my name again, closer still, directly behind me. I tucked myself in behind the thick, straight trunk of a towering tree, bunched my fingers into tight, tight fists, and waited.

For almost a minute I stood there, my legs cramping painfully as I struggled to stay motionless and hidden. My breath rattled in and out, surely loud enough to give me away. I could do nothing to quieten it, though, and when I heard the murderer's footsteps thudding closer and closer, each breath came louder still.

When the rustling of the grass was almost beside me, I leapt out of my hiding place, head down, shoulder out. The thing wearing Ameena's body let out a gasp of shock. It couldn't move fast enough to dodge my charge, and its ribs made a satisfying *crunch* as my shoulder slammed against them.

The pain from my injuries was nearly overwhelming. It

stopped me concentrating, made it impossible for me to use my powers. That suited me fine. I didn't want to use the power. I wanted to pound on the monster, punish it with my bare hands, make it realise the mistake it had made by taking Ameena away from me.

I would make the Crowmaster beg, make him plead with me to spare him. And when he'd done that – when he'd wept and screamed and cried out for me to let him live, I'd say just one word.

I'd say 'No'.

My charge didn't take as much out of it as I'd hoped. It twisted Ameena's body, deflecting the brunt of my attack and sending us both spinning down on to the forest floor.

'Have you gone *mental*?' Ameena's voice demanded, as we both scrabbled to get up. The Crowmaster was still trying to trick me, still trying to make me believe I was attacking my friend. I blocked it out and focused on the fight.

We were halfway to our feet when I drove my fist hard against what had once been Ameena's cheek, dropping down and letting my weight add power to the punch.

The Crowmaster glared at me through Ameena's eyes. 'Right,' he said, still sounding exactly like her, 'that's it.'

A jab to my throat left me gasping for air. I was too busy choking even to try to defend myself when the thing in Ameena's skin leapt on top of me, pressing a knee hard against my chest. I fought hard, kicking and pushing, but the tightness in my throat and the pressure on my chest kept me pinned down.

'Spectacular a hissy fit as this is, we don't have time for it,' her voice growled.

'I'll kill you,' I hissed. 'I swear I'll kill you for this.'

'For *what*? What are you spazzing out about now?'

'You don't care, do you?' I snarled. Tears ran in different directions down both sides of my head, pooling in my ears. 'You took her away from me, and you don't give a damn! She meant something to me – *she meant everything to me* – and you used her like… like…'

I wilted beneath the puzzled gaze of those eyes, so brown as to be almost black. 'You didn't have to kill her,' I mumbled. 'You didn't have to kill Ameena.'

'Er… hello? What? Listen, kiddo, I don't know what you think has happened, but I'm pretty sure I'm not dead.' She glanced up into the darkness lurking between the trees. 'Not yet, anyway.'

Kiddo. She'd called me 'kiddo'. I hated it when she called me 'kiddo'. She *always* called me 'kiddo'.

But no, it was a trick. He was messing with my head.

'You're not her,' I said through clenched teeth. 'You're the Crowmaster.'

'I'm not the Crowmaster!' she retorted, almost smiling at the suggestion.

She didn't smile for long. The spindly fingers crept like an insect through her hair, yanking her head backwards before either of us could react. The weight lifted from my chest in a sharp, sudden jerk. Ameena bit her lip, trying to resist screaming or swearing. Or both.

'That's right, you ain't,' the scarecrow said, his face split into a grin, that horrible laugh of his hissing in Ameena's ear. *SS-SS-SS-SS-SS!* '*I* am!'

I don't remember getting up. One moment I was flat on the ground, and the next I was standing there in front of them both, the pain that had been ravaging my body a rapidly fading memory.

The Crowmaster had one of his pets perched on his shoulder – a fat, ugly brute with blood on its beak. Its head twitched at every little movement I made, and I knew the scarecrow was watching me through the crow's eyes.

Ameena was staying unusually quiet, and I only had to glance at her to realise why. One of the Crowmaster's long black fingernails was pressed against her throat. It dug in deeper with every breath she took, until a trickle of red crept down her neck.

'Let her go.'

'Now why would I go and do a thing like that?' the scarecrow sneered.

'It's me you want, not her. Let her go.'

'That's one mighty big head you got there, boy,' he hissed. 'Some folks might think you're somethin' special, but me? I don't care one little bit.' He hocked up a mouthful of black saliva and spat it on to the ground at my feet. 'I let this one go on purpose, see? Thought it'd be a real hoot to let you think she was me. Thought you might slit her throat and bleed her dry, or at least beat on her until she stopped beating back.'

He pressed his talon harder against Ameena's throat, making her eyes bulge. 'But instead what do you do? You cry like a baby and get your ass whupped by a girl. Man, that was a disappointing moment.'

'What is it you want?' I asked.

'I already got what I want, boy,' he smirked. 'Thanks to your daddy I got me a Get Outta Hell Free card. Now all I gotta do is kill you and there ain't no way hell can follow me here.'

'Then let Ameena go,' I said. 'You don't have to hurt her.'

'Oh sure, I don't *have* to,' he grinned, 'but I bet it'll be all kinds of fun.'

His empty eye sockets widened and that flesh-crawling laugh hissed from his wide cavernous mouth. He yanked harder on Ameena's hair until she couldn't help but scream. His hand drew back, the stupidly elongated fingers splaying out, the claws extending to their full terrifying length, aiming for Ameena's exposed throat.

He was halfway through the movement, too far into it to stop suddenly. That was my cue. Clenching my fist, I did something I never anticipated I'd ever find myself doing.

I punched a crow in the face.

The Crowmaster may have been expecting me to attack him, but he wasn't prepared for me hitting the bird. Nor, it seems, was the bird. It flipped backwards off its master's shoulder, squawking and flapping as it tried to slow its fall.

Still seeing through the crow's eyes, the Crowmaster became instantly disorientated. His ragged nails swished narrowly past Ameena's throat, throwing them both off balance. Ameena twisted her shoulder into him and bent at the waist, letting his momentum carry him up and over her back.

Even before the scarecrow hit the ground, Ameena bounded over to where the bird had landed on the forest floor. Lifting her boot, she brought it down hard on the crow's head.

'Have some of *that*!' she cried triumphantly, before a sudden fluttering filled the forest behind us.

'Move!' Ameena cried, catching me by the arm. Before I knew what was happening, I was fleeing again, hurrying through the trees, ducking and jumping and weaving through a denser and denser jungle of roots and weeds and thin, tangling branches.

That sound – that rhythmic rippling of rapid applause – was growing louder, the birds quickly closing the gap between us.

Ameena moved through the trees like a shark through water, cutting effortlessly through the forest and pulling away from me with every bound. The mass of pain that I'd temporarily managed to forget about now came rushing back, making my head throb and my chest burn and my limbs turn achingly heavy.

I would have given up then, I'm almost certain. With the crows screeching behind me and my legs buckling beneath me, I would have surely collapsed to the ground and let them do whatever it was they were going to do.

I would have died there in the clawing darkness of the woods, had I not seen the clearing through a gap in the trees. 'Over there!' I shouted, my voice little more than a loud croak. Ameena turned and followed my finger, which was pointing ahead and to her right.

It took her a moment to realise what she was looking at, but then she banked sharply and began to run faster. I was already crashing after her, and together we hurried towards the clearing.

And towards the towering mast that loomed imposingly at its heart.

Chapter Nineteen

THE MAST

'What now?' Ameena barked as I entered the clearing just a few paces behind her.

I didn't reply, partly because I was too out of breath to speak, but mostly because I didn't know what to say. I had no idea what we should do next.

The mast was much larger than I'd expected. It almost filled the width of the clearing, and stretched way up into the dusky darkness above our heads. From a distance it had seemed to shine with a near-supernatural silvery sheen. Up close, it was a dull gun-metal grey, with no sign of the gleam it had appeared to possess.

I tried to tell myself it didn't make any difference. What mattered were the components of the mast – the dishes, the antennae, the big knobbly bits that stuck out of the side – not how shiny it was. And yet, even though I knew this, the lack of that near-magical sparkle caused my heart to sink, and made me wonder if the whole plan wasn't doomed to failure.

The birds were still flocking after us, now just a few metres from the clearing. An image of their vicious beaks snapped into focus in my mind's eye, closely followed by visions of Marion and Toto's remains. *Both* Totos.

Once again I found myself wondering about the dog that had come leaping to my rescue from… well, from nowhere. That big, powerful, savage animal that had appeared at just the right moment to save me from death, just like the mattress had.

But once again I had no time to dwell on the mystery of the two Totos. The crows were swarming into the clearing now, and if we didn't move fast the dog's rescue – and death – would have been in vain.

'Into the middle,' I yelped, already running, 'beneath the tower!'

'I heard these things give you brain tumours,' she said,

moving forward, but not quite running.

'Really?' I snapped, hurrying past her. 'Well I know for a fact *those* things tear your face off and eat it. Take your pick.'

Ameena overtook me before I'd finished the sentence. She stopped almost exactly in the centre of the space beneath the mast. By the time she spun round I was beside her, gripping the sleeve of her jacket for no reason other than fear.

A bubble of panic formed in my throat when I realised the birds weren't slowing. They raced in our direction, a wide stream of black, flowing from the trees and heading directly towards us.

'Do something!'

I pushed down the pain, forgot the fact that fifty per cent of my face was so smashed up it looked like mashed potato. The birds were coming, and I was the only one who could—

'They're turning!' Ameena yelled, before I could even attempt anything. 'Check it out!'

She was right. As the line of birds reached the mast it split in two, each half arcing around the outside of the structure until they crossed paths at the other side. They didn't slow down then, just kept flying around and around, one half moving in one direction, the other half taking the opposite route, criss-crossing their way around the mast.

Faster and faster they flew, until the sheer speed of their flight made it impossible to follow any one individual bird. Faster still they went, moving fluidly, somehow able to avoid crashing into all the other birds racing in the opposite direction.

'What are they doing?' Ameena asked. She was clinging to my arm now, as tightly as I clung to hers.

'I... I don't know,' I confessed. 'I thought the mast would send them crazy, make them fly away. Like the phone did.'

'But it isn't.'

'Isn't it?' I whispered. 'I'm not sure. They're not coming in here. They're not trying to get at us.'

'Probably heard about the brain tumours,' Ameena muttered.

'Maybe...' I looked up at the massive, towering structure above our heads. From directly below it seemed impossibly big, like some giant metal dinosaur. I wondered how many calls it could handle at once.

And then a terrible thought hit me. The mast was up here on a hillside in the middle of nowhere, miles from anything even resembling civilisation. What if the birds weren't being driven back because nobody was making a call? The phone had only scattered the crows when it had started to ring – the signal, I guessed, somehow breaking the Crowmaster's hold on them as it travelled through the air.

If no one made a call, then would there be a signal from the mast? Would there be anything to stop the birds?

I hurriedly told Ameena my theory. Her face seemed to crumple before I was half finished. She glanced at the circle of screeching death that surrounded us, and not for the first time that night I could see real, raw fear in her eyes.

'They're not scared to come in,' she said, realising the same thing I had just half a second before her. 'They're keeping us trapped. They're keeping us in here.' She tore her gaze from the birds and turned to me. There was no hope in her wide, dark eyes. 'He's coming. He's coming for us.'

'Listen,' I said, trying to sound like I believed what I was about to say, 'I have an idea.'

I could tell from the way she looked at me that she'd heard the doubt in my voice. Still, we both knew we were beyond even the clutching at straws stage. What we needed now was a miracle.

'OK,' she said, nodding slowly. 'Spill.'

I took a short breath, swallowed once, and then put the sentence out there.

'I think I created that dog.'

She blinked. Whatever insanity she had expected to emerge from my mouth, I had obviously surpassed it.

'It sounds crazy, yes, and I don't know if I believe it myself, but he just kind of appeared from nowhere, like, well, like Mr Mumbles and Caddie did back at the house. And there was a mattress too; I think I made that, and—'

'Do it,' Ameena said, cutting me off mid-babble. 'Whatever you're planning, do it.' She stole another look at the wall of birds. 'Although it's going to take one mean dog to get through all that.'

'I wasn't thinking about a dog,' I told her. I could feel my cheeks flush red at the sheer ridiculousness of what I was saying. 'I was going to see if I could make a... a mobile phone.'

She blinked again and her head made a very slight spasming movement, as if she was fighting back the urge to laugh. 'Right,' she nodded. 'Good. Go for it.' She squeezed her lips between her fingertips, trying to stop herself saying anything else. She failed miserably. 'Just make sure you top it up first.'

I ignored the jibe. Ameena and I both knew this was our last chance. All I had to do to save us was create a complex piece of telecommunications equipment from thin air. That was it. Simple.

Yeah, right.

Still, I had to try. I held out my left hand, palm facing me, fingers curled around a handset I had not even begun to imagine. As the birds whipped around us and my head throbbed like it was about to implode, I closed my eyes and tried to paint a picture with my mind.

'If I can make a dog, I can make a phone,' I said, steeling my determination.

'There's a sentence I never thought I'd hear out loud.'

I ignored that comment too. All that mattered was the phone. The phone I was trying to imagine nestled in the palm of my left hand. The phone that would save our lives.

Slowly, almost cautiously, I felt the first tingle inch across my scalp. It moved at such a crawl it took all my willpower to avoid concentrating on it and accidentally whisking myself off to the Darkest Corners. If it came to it, that place might prove to be a last-chance escape route, but going there would only delay the inevitable. Besides, I knew from experience that there could be something even worse waiting for us on the other side.

I screwed up my face and tried to dredge up the details of the phone Mum had given me. It had been black, or maybe a very dark blue. The buttons were grey with... were the numbers yellow? Or white?

Ignoring the detail, I concentrated on the phone's shape, and how it had felt in my hand. Solid, but not too heavy. How long was the casing? I felt sweat on my brow. How wide was the screen? I cursed myself for not having paid more attention.

Despite my uncertainties, the tingling filled my head. I heard Ameena whistle softly, before she blurted, 'Something happening,' in a voice filled with wonder.

I kept concentrating, feeling something take form in the crook of my palm. I didn't open my eyes, but maintained my focus, trying to pin down an image of the phone, trying to remember every last detail.

When next Ameena spoke, the amazement was gone from her tone. Her voice was flat and deflated. 'Oh.'

Blinking open my eyes, I looked down at my hand. There was a phone there. Of sorts. It looked like three or four different phones melted together.

It was as wide as it was long, with a jumbled mish-mash of buttons scattered apparently at random across the front. The screen was shaped like an upside-down letter L, but tapered to a point at one end. The casing itself seemed to be made of a number of different materials – from shiny black plastic to dull chrome – with no obvious joins between them.

I knew the phone wasn't going to work. It was too distorted, too deformed to be operational. Also, I'd forgotten to give it an "on" button.

'Well, it nearly worked,' Ameena said, trying to sound encouraging, 'which, I'll be honest, is a damn sight more than I expected.'

On the one hand I was devastated – the phone had been our only chance, and I'd screwed it up. But on the other hand I was amazed – amazed that I'd managed to create something out of nothing, just by thinking about it. OK, it wasn't perfect, but it was *there*. It *existed*, and that set me wondering just how powerful these abilities of mine actually were.

Ameena tugged on my sleeve and I looked up from the useless brick in my hand. It took me a moment, but then I saw him, standing just inside the circle of birds. His empty eyes were trained on us both. Another crow sat perched on his shoulder, watching us on his behalf.

He began to prowl around the mast, but never venturing beneath it. And all the while, the crows flew by behind him, a blurred wall of living black.

He didn't speak, just stared at us. We watched him pad back and forth, like a tiger waiting on feeding time at the zoo. The only difference was we were the ones inside the cage, not him.

'Don't get me wrong, I'm not complaining,' Ameena said in a whisper, 'but why isn't he coming in?'

'Maybe because...' I began, but the sentence ended there. I had no idea why he wasn't coming for us. Nothing made sense any more. 'It must have something to do with the mast,' I guessed. 'Maybe the signal's stronger under it or something.'

'But I thought you said it didn't send out any signals unless someone made a call?'

'Yeah, but I'm not a mobile phone engineer, am I?' I said, with more venom than I meant. 'Maybe it's something like that, or maybe he's just claustrophobic, or maybe he heard you talking about brain tumours. At this point your guess is as good as mine.'

'Fine. Then care to hazard a guess at what he's doing now?'

The Crowmaster was no longer pacing. He was stretching up with his elongated arms, wrapping his spindly fingers around the first of the twenty or so horizontal metal struts that ran up all four sides of the mast. The gap between each bar must've been over two metres, but the length of his limbs meant he was able to haul himself up with ease.

We watched him pull himself on to the first strut. It wasn't until he reached for the second that we realised he was climbing the mast.

I let my gaze overtake him, craning my neck and tilting my head until I could see what the Crowmaster was climbing towards. And I knew, in a flash, we were done for.

'I was right, it's something to do with the signals,' I said, so quietly I could barely hear myself over the screeching of the birds. 'And he's going to stop them.

'He's going to smash the transmitter!'

Chapter Twenty

THE MONSTER WITHIN

The wind cut like a knife. It sliced through my T-shirt and nipped at my lungs. In an attempt to keep my internal organs from freezing, all the blood was rushing from my fingers, making it difficult to hold on to the icy metal rungs of the ladder.

For the first fifteen metres or so the trees had shielded us from the worst of the chill factor, but up here – past what I guessed must be twenty-five metres – we were completely exposed to punishing gusts of the harsh January wind.

The ladder ran up the inside of the mast, just a metre or two from the horizontal struts the Crowmaster was clambering up. He was faster than I was, but the ladder was an easier climb, and despite the loss of feeling in my fingers, I was gaining steadily.

Ameena, though, was catching up even more quickly. As usual, she had acted before I had, launching herself up the ladder before I had even realised the need to climb. I'd quickly followed, making a lot of noise about her letting me go first, but privately hoping she didn't take the offer up.

When we'd faced Caddie and Raggy Maggie, I'd been amazed at how quickly Ameena could climb a rope ladder, but that was nothing compared to how she darted up this one.

Her movements were fluid and graceful, giving the illusion she was hardly hurrying at all. With each step, though, I fell further and further behind, and even when I worked my aching limbs to their limits, I still only barely managed to keep pace.

She was eight or nine metres ahead of me now, just three or four below the Crowmaster. If she was scared, she wasn't showing it, not even slowing as she began to draw level with the scarecrow's monstrous form.

The sky was a little brighter up here, away from the

shadowy canopy of the trees. Through the covering of cloud I could see a hazy patch of light, just above the horizon. Over to my right, the embers of Marion's house glowed brightly, rebelling against the dusk. Down below, I could still hear the birds circling around the mast's base.

The Crowmaster made another leap upwards, pulling away from Ameena. She climbed faster, hands and feet moving in perfect harmony, regaining the ground she had lost.

It was a race to the transmitter, and they were neck and neck. For the first time since starting to climb, though, I wondered what we were going to do when we got there.

A blast of icy wind hit me face on, pushing me backwards away from the ladder. For one heart-stopping moment I thought I was going to fall, but my fingers held their grip, and I was moving again in moments.

I looked up at Ameena and cried out in triumph. She was pulling ahead of the scarecrow, leaving him behind. She was going to beat him to the top, although I still didn't know if she'd planned any further ahead than that.

'Keep going!' I shouted. 'You're doing it!'

The sound of my voice made her hesitate. She looked down at me. 'What?'

'I said— Look out!'

He swung out at her, one arm holding on to the mast's frame, the other held at full stretch. His fist jabbed between the rungs of the ladder, slamming into the top of her head with such force that I heard it over the whistling of the wind.

And then he was back on his perch, hands already reaching for the next bar. And Ameena...

Ameena was falling.

She dropped backwards off the ladder, arms out by her sides, hands clawing at the air. I gripped on to a rung with one hand, swung out just as the Crowmaster had done. Her fingers touched mine, our eyes briefly met, but then she was gone, plummeting past me on the way to the ground far below.

'Catch her, catch her, catch her!' I screamed to the world in general, my hand still stretched out for her. Lightning exploded in my head, blindingly bright, but gone in a fraction of a second.

A dark shape broke through the wall of birds, rocketing across the gap and wrapping its stubby arms around Ameena's back. The wind nipped my eyes, bringing tears, so that I couldn't see the figure in any detail. I could see, though, that it was short and stunted, but with a pair of feathery wings on its back, like some kind of deformed angel.

I watched – barely able to believe what I was seeing – as the flying *thing* dropped Ameena awkwardly on to the grass, banked left, then punched its way through the circling crows. I looked for it, but it didn't emerge on the other side of the birds.

Ameena got up and spun on the spot, looking for whatever it was that had saved her. She shouted up to me, but I was too far away to make out the words. The sheer amazement in her tone told me she was OK, though, which left me free to concentrate on catching the Crowmaster.

I gritted my teeth and pushed upwards. A large, drum-like dish loomed above my head. The scarecrow had almost reached it. There was no way I could beat him to it, but if I worked my legs hard enough, I could get there right behind him.

The ladder vibrated a little in my hand, and I knew without looking that Ameena had rejoined the chase. It was reassuring to know she was coming, but she was too far away to make much difference. It was me and the Crowmaster now, and part of me – the small part that wasn't quaking with fear – wouldn't have wanted it any other way.

He was waiting for me at the top, hanging on to the curve of the dish, drumming his fingers against its side. I hooked an arm around the ladder, expecting him to swing for me at any moment, just as he'd done to Ameena.

But he didn't. Instead he smiled and said, 'Sure took your time, boy.'

I didn't know what to say at first. The crow on his shoulder hopped up on to his head, then down on to the other shoulder, watching me all the way.

'What?' I asked. It wasn't the heroic retort I'd been

looking for, but he'd caught me off guard and it was all I could think to say. I tried to pull it back. 'I'm not letting you smash that dish.'

SS-SS-SS-SS. That laugh again. God, I hated that laugh.

'Smash it? I ain't gonna smash it, boy. Why would I smash it?'

'Because it can stop you,' I said, although even I couldn't miss the uncertainty in my voice. 'Because of the interference.'

His face – or what was left of it – took on an expression of genuine puzzlement. 'I ain't got the first clue what you're talking about.'

'The way you control the birds,' I said. 'You send some sort of signal, the same way mobile phones do. That's how you do it. But the signal from a *real* mobile phone messes your signal up. Right?'

'Yup.'

That surprised me. 'I am?' I said. 'I mean, right. I am. That's why you're going to smash this, to stop any more signals interfering with yours.'

'I told you, boy, I ain't gonna smash nothin'.'

My mind raced. He'd reached the dish well before me. If he had wanted to break it he could have done so before I'd been close enough to stop him. So why hadn't he? Why come all the way up here if he wasn't going to smash it?

I looked down. Ameena was still far below. The birds were still circling around the outside of the mast. The clearing was...

Wait.

The Crowmaster's feet were on the horizontal strut, his hands were on the dish, but he was leaning backwards, away from the mast. He was on the outside, just like the birds.

And the dish. The dish was pointing outwards.

'You didn't come below the mast because there's no signal there,' I said, the truth finally dawning. 'The dish itself doesn't interfere with your control at all. You need the dish. You use it to broadcast the signal, and the dish doesn't point underneath the mast, it only points outwards.'

'Well, check out the big brain on you, boy,' the Crowmaster sneered. 'Give yourself a pat on the back.' He held up a gnarled hand. 'No, wait, don't do that, you might fall off, and that'd really screw up my plan.'

I felt the colour drain from my face. 'What plan?'

'You think you found your way here by accident, boy?' he cackled. 'I been leading you here right from the start. I planted them seeds in your head, made you think that little telephone of yours could hurt me. In the bedroom. Down in the mud after I tossed you out the window. It was all an act, boy. All an act to make you think you had a way to stop me.'

'No,' I said weakly. 'That's not true.'

'Kidnapping your girl, getting my babies to chase you in just the exact right direction – all this time I been leading you right here. Right to this moment.'

'Why?' I asked, my throat suddenly tight.

'So I could do *this*.'

The crow on his shoulder squawked, drawing my attention away from the Crowmaster himself. His arm uncoiled like a whip. His hand was on my head, the palm flat across my hair. Then came five sharp, blistering pains.

I threw up one hand, trying to break his grip, but his claw-like fingernails were through my skin, pressing in hard against my skull.

I felt the power surge through me, crackling across my scalp, surging to the points where the scarecrow's fingers met my head.

'Yeah!' he screeched. 'Yeehaw!'

The dark hollows of his eyes were lit up a bright, brilliant blue. Tendrils of electricity crawled across his whole body, standing out like bulging, varicose veins.

'It's incredible,' he crowed, 'the power! The things you can do, boy. The things you can do!'

I was screaming now, one arm still wrapped around the ladder, the other clutching his wrist. It felt solid, like a plank of wood, and I couldn't do a thing to break the grip.

'Now,' he grinned, holding up his other hand. Energy danced between his fingertips. 'Watch the birdie.'

He jammed his hand into the centre of the dish. At once, the veins of electricity arced along his arm, spreading out like a spider-web across the dish's blank grey surface.

The first flurry of movement happened in seconds. They rose from the trees a mile or so to our left, one at a time at first, then in groups of five, then ten or more, until they hung above the forest like a dark fog.

On all sides the crows began to rise up above the treetops, screeching and cawing as they homed in on the Crowmaster's amplified signal.

In the distance, other birds had appeared over the crest of a hill. Others still swooped towards us from the fields way over on my right. In moments there were hundreds of them – thousands – all drawing together and darkening half of the sky.

'I almost didn't believe them things your daddy told me,' he sniggered, watching as yet more and more of the birds joined the growing flock. 'Not until I saw it for myself. I did think about just killing you, but then I thought "Why not *use* him instead?".' He leaned in until his mouth was by my ear. 'You're gonna be my battery, boy. I'm gonna drain every last drop of that power and use it to send my babies out into the world.

'I wonder,' he whispered, barely able to hold back his

laughter, 'how your momma will scream when they're tearing at her insides? Will she holler your name? I'll be sure to let you know.'

I smashed my fist against him again. Again he shrugged it off.

'Don't look so glum, boy. You know what they say – it's better to light a candle than to curse the darkness. Try to look on the bright side.' He pulled me in closer and flashed his rotting teeth in my face. 'I'm gonna keep you alive for a very long time.'

Light a candle. The phrase buzzed through my skull. *Light a candle, light a candle, light a candle.*

I dug into my back pocket and found what I was looking for. The metal top of the lighter sprung open as I brought it up and flicked the metal wheel, sparking it up.

A flash of panic whipped across the Crowmaster's face. I flicked the lighter again, but the wind stole the spark away. Before I could try for a third time, his fingernails slashed across my knuckles, knocking the lighter from my grip.

It sailed off towards the middle of the mast and dropped out of sight, taking my hopes with it. The self-satisfied smirk returned to the scarecrow's face.

'She made me watch that movie too many times for me to be caught out by a lighter,' he told me. 'You gotta be quicker'n that, boy.'

'I... made... a... dog!'

The Crowmaster spluttered a laugh and pulled back, his bright blue eyes boring into mine. 'Say what now?'

The pain was almost unbearable. It started in my head, but washed through me like acid, until it felt like all my insides were swishing around my feet. I could feel my power flowing out of me, draining away, but it felt like something was flowing back in at the same time.

Whether it was my abilities trying to save my life again, or whether I was somehow siphoning off some of the Crowmaster's regeneration ability, I'll never know. But as we hung there from the ladder, dangerously far from the ground, my battered body began to heal. I couldn't see the wounds closing over, but I could feel them, and as each one sealed shut, I could feel my strength returning. And the stronger I became, the clearer I could think.

I had a plan. A plan that was going to work.

'Do you have... *any* idea how hard it is t-to make a dog?' I hissed.

The area above the scarecrow's eyes furrowed down. 'Yet again, son, I don't have the first damn clue what you're—'

'It's really hard,' I grimaced. 'There's the head to think about, then the... then the legs and the tail.' The Crowmaster was looking more and more bewildered, and as his frown deepened, the pain racking my body lessened a shade. 'Lungs, liver, brain, eyes, it's not easy making a dog. And I made one. I made other stuff too. People, even.'

'*So?*'

'So if I can make something as complicated as a dog,' I said, grabbing hold of his arm, 'I can *definitely* make something much simpler. Like a flame.'

A wisp of smoke curled up around my fingertips and a shudder travelled the length of the Crowmaster's body. The blue light faded from the dark holes of his eyes as the straw of his arm began to smoulder and burn.

'No!' he howled. 'No, no, no, no!'

The fire caught hold properly, forcing me to pull back from the sudden searing heat. The movement tore his arm in half and he gave a scream – not of pain, but of shock and fear.

I pulled the hand with its burning stump from my head and hurled it away from the mast, towards where the huge cloud of crows was almost upon us. I watched them for a moment, mesmerised by their sheer number.

When I turned back to the Crowmaster the right side of his body from his shoulder to his hip was aflame. He twisted and writhed on the ladder, as if trying somehow to shake the flames away.

'Get me out, get me out,' he cried, but his voice sounded different – not just his tone, but the actual voice itself. 'Get me out of this thing!'

Strands of burning straw were carried away on the wind, drifting off into the darkening sky. The fire consumed the scarecrow's entire body, swallowing his head and his chest, before spreading down to his legs.

As the straw was eaten away, it began to reveal another figure lurking within the Crowmaster's frame. He was much smaller than the Crowmaster had been. Smaller than me, even, but with the wrinkled face of an ancient old man.

His hair was black and oily, like the feathers of a crow. He wore a white shirt and a red waistcoat with matching red trousers, all of which seemed completely unharmed by the fire.

He kicked and thrashed the last of the burning straw away, then grabbed for a rung of the ladder with both pudgy hands. 'My costume,' he wailed. 'My favourite costume.'

I looked down at him, too shocked to respond.

'My costume! You ruined my favourite costume!' he screamed, froth foaming on his cracked and withered lips.

'Wait, so you're... you're Joe Crow,' I realised. 'The *real* Joe Crow. And that was Marion's missing scarecrow outfit.'

I shook my head. 'I've been running from a midget in fancy dress.'

'Shut up!' he snarled, opening his mouth to reveal two rows of shark-like teeth. 'I'll rip your heart out and swallow it whole!'

'OK, a *grumpy* midget in fancy dress.'

'I'm the Crowmaster!' he howled, stamping his stubby foot on the ladder like an angry toddler. 'I'm the Crowmaster!'

I looked behind him. 'You told me you controlled the birds through fear,' I said.

'That's right, that's right!' he spat. 'So?'

My grip on the ladder tightened. 'I don't think they're afraid of you any more.'

And at that, all hell broke loose.

The birds howled around us, swooping and banking and dive-bombing with outstretched claws and snapping beaks. This time, though, it wasn't me they were targeting.

'Get them off, get them off!' Joe Crow pleaded. He swung out with an arm, trying to scare them away, wailing,

'Make them stop, boy! Make them stop.'

'You should never have come to my world,' I told him, shouting to make myself heard above the racket of the birds and his own screams.

I could barely even see him beneath the thrashing mountain of feathers. The birds were relentless in their attack, taking their bloody revenge on the man who had manipulated them. I couldn't have stopped them, and after everything he'd done to me and the people I cared about, I wasn't sure I wanted to.

'You should have stayed in the Darkest Corners,' I shouted, just before his grip finally slipped and he plunged backwards towards the ground. A cloud of birds swallowed him before he was even halfway down, and, with a sudden jolt, his howls of agony abruptly stopped.

'I mean, didn't anyone ever tell you?' I spoke into the wind, 'there's no place like home.'

'Good grief, that was insane! In. Sane.'

Ameena had finally joined me at the top of the ladder.

We stood on the same rung, leaning towards opposite sides, our arms wrapped around the ladder's frame. I was exhausted, but with my injuries healed up I was feeling stronger than I'd felt in hours. Even my shattered nose had repaired itself, although the five deep scratches on my scalp where the Crowmaster's claws had caught me hadn't gone anywhere.

Ameena and I had watched the birds drift off one by one, until there was barely a handful of them left. Of Joe Crow there was no sign, but even from up here the grass looked slick with puddles of red.

'Tell me about it,' I nodded, suddenly feeling very queasy.

'I'd like to see him try to get up from that!'

'I wouldn't.'

Ameena nodded. 'No, suppose not.'

We stood way up there for a few moments, not saying anything, just lost in our own thoughts. When Ameena did speak again, her voice was light, as if the past few hours were already forgotten. 'So,' she began, 'what now?'

'I need to go and see Mum. Make sure she's OK.'

Ameena nodded again, but didn't say anything. We both looked over to the smouldering remains of Marion's house. For a long time all we did was watch the embers burn.

'People are going to ask questions,' she said, at last.

It was my turn to nod and stay silent.

'They're going to place you at the scene.'

I gave another nod and scratched one of the claw marks on my head. It was starting to itch.

'I don't think they'll believe the evil imaginary friends thing.'

'Doubt it,' I agreed.

'You might end up doing bird,' she said, and then broke into a laugh. Only the puzzled expression on my face stopped her. *'Doing bird,'* she repeated. 'As in *going to jail.'*

I winced, more at the joke than the thought of prison. 'Oh.'

'Get it?'

'Got it, thanks.'

'Genius,' she grinned. 'Right, let's go.' She moved to take a step down the ladder, but stopped with one foot in mid-air. When she raised her head to look at me there was still a smile on her face, but it was an uncertain one. 'Oh, and… um… thanks.'

'For what?'

She glanced down at the ground, then back up to me. Her eyes were narrowed and her brow was creased, as if she was doing some tricky mental calculation. 'You know, for the…' she paused and gave a slight shake of her head. 'That thing that caught me,' she frowned, 'that *was* a flying monkey, right?'

I gazed past Ameena, down to where I'd seen the winged figure snatch her from the air. My stomach tightened, ejecting a snort of nervous laughter out through my nose.

My powers were growing, that much was clear. But my control over them wasn't keeping pace. The abilities were unpredictable – maybe dangerously so. I had no idea what

I was doing half the time, never mind how I was doing it. That was worrying.

But still, a flying monkey. Marion would have been proud.

'Any time,' I said, and together we began the long, tiring climb back down to Earth.